the
HEIST

THERESA SEDERHOLT

the
HEIST

chapter
ONE

Amelia

TODAY IS THE DAY I'VE BEEN DREADING FOR TWENTY years. It's the day I head into court and finally declare my husband Peter dead. It really is a double-edged sword. Part of me wants to close the chapter and move on, the other part of me wants to know why Peter disappeared without a trace. Twenty years ago, he went out to the store to satisfy one of my many pregnancy cravings. He drove off into the night and never came back. I was seven months pregnant and no family of my own to fall back on, being a product of the foster care system from the time I was four. His parents died in a car accident the year before. Everything was solely on me. I called the police and filed a missing person's report, but they didn't take me seriously. They were of the school of thought that he didn't want all the responsibility of raising a family. I knew that wasn't the case, but they wouldn't listen. So, every week for twenty years, I would go to the police department and check on his case. After he was missing for ten years, I was able to file a motion to declare him dead, but I had to wait another ten years to declare him legally dead. So basically, I put my life on hold for twenty years. I raised my daughter Emma alone. I had to work two jobs to support us: a clerical job for the Department of Motor Vehicles and cleaning office buildings at night. Pretty boring, but I did whatever I could to make a somewhat normal life for Emma. She's in college now trying to find her own way. I'm grateful that Peter thought to take out a life insurance policy. At least the money from the policy will come in handy for her student loans.

Emma wanted to come with me today, but I asked her not to. There is no reason for her to mourn the death of a man she didn't know. I never hid the facts about her father's disappearance from her. I've always believed in complete transparency with everything in life. I never wanted her to go out into the world with rose-colored glasses on. I take one more look in the mirror, swipe my lips with my Charlotte Tilbury's Pillow Talk lip gloss, adjust my imaginary crown, and head out the door.

I don't know what I was expecting. Maybe some sort of condolences or something. With the slam of a gavel and a stamp on a death certificate, Peter Mach is no more. The whole process took ten minutes. Twenty years of my life put on hold for ten minutes in the court house. As I make my way out to the street, I run into Peter's friend, Mitch Stein. I haven't seen him in so many years; what are the odds I would see him today—the day he's declared legally dead?

"Amelia, oh my God, you haven't changed in years. You still look beautiful as ever."

"Twenty years, Mitch, to be exact. Thank you. You haven't changed, either." My foster mom always told me *"If you can be anything, be kind."* Sometimes the years are not the kindest. He's still a handsome man, but I guess I'm remembering him in his youth. "I officially had Peter declared legally dead today." I don't know why I felt the need to tell him that.

"Wow, it was so long ago. How is Emma doing?" He moves from foot to foot, looking everywhere but at me. Can you say extremely uncomfortable?

"Emma is great. She's at Northwestern University. How's your family?"

"Becky and I got divorced and Brook is in her senior year at Boston University."

"Oh, I'm sorry to hear that. About Becky, that is. Well, I've got to get going." *Very awkward.*

"Do you want to get together for a drink sometime?"

Not really but I don't want to be rude. "Sure." I pull out my phone and we exchange numbers before I hightail it out of there. Now I just hope he doesn't call me.

chapter
TWO

Amelia

AS I SIT ON THE SUBWAY STARING AT PETER'S DEATH certificate, I realize I am a single woman now. For twenty years I had casual dates but, technically, I was still married. I was young and the guys my age were looking for a future, not a future put on hold. Anyway, I've been single for so long, I don't think I want to get married. I can sell my house, but where would I go? I can't follow my daughter. I mean, who knows where she will end up? Besides, I read someplace that following your children around the country is bad for them.

The train comes to a stop and I begin the trek home. My phone chirps with a new text message. I retrieve it from my purse to discover that it's Mitch.

Mitch: It was so great to see you again. Would you like to get together for a drink tonight?

What really gets my goat is when Peter first went missing, his friends were here all the time. Then after about three months, I never heard from them again. Now Mitch wants to go for drinks on the same day Peter was declared dead?

Me: Wow, you didn't waste any time. Obviously today isn't a great day for me. Maybe another time.

Mitch: Amelia, it's just drinks.

It doesn't seem that he's going to take "no" for an answer. I stare at my phone for what seems like forever but, in reality, it's not. I quickly reply.

Me: How about tomorrow?

Mitch: Great. I'll pick you up at eight.

Me: See you then.

I'm not going to put off the inevitable; one drink and I'm done.

I live in the Flatbush section of Brooklyn, New York. I had a car but when Peter left that night, he took it with him. It showed up six months later torched but Peter wasn't in it. Just another mystery that surrounds his disappearance. I had no money to replace the car, so I quickly got used to taking the trains and walking wherever I needed to go. Besides, the expense of a vehicle in New York City is insane. I promised Emma I would call her when everything was over. I check my phone, and with the time difference, she should just be finishing her chemical engineering class.

"Hey, Mom, how did everything go? Are you okay? I wish you would have let me come home like I wanted to."

"Slow down, Emma, I'm fine. The whole process took

ten minutes. It's done, and we need to look toward the future. How are you doing?"

"Mom, trying to deflect the conversation back toward me is not going to make it go away. It's okay to mourn him now that you finally got closure."

"Emma, it will take a lot more than the slap of the gavel and a rubber stamp to give me the closure I need. Look, let's put that aside for now. What I wanted to talk to you about is the house. I was thinking of selling it. How do you feel about it?"

"Where will you go?" I can hear the angst in her voice. Maybe it's too soon for her to even think about this, but that's all I've done for twenty years—think about how to move on.

"I think I want to go someplace that's more like the country . . . you know, not the concrete jungle that I'm in now. If you don't want me to sell it, I won't." I know it's her childhood home and even though she didn't know her father, it's a good memory that I'm proud I made for her.

"It's up to you mom, but don't do anything until I get home this weekend. We can talk about it then."

"Okay, I'm going to call the insurance company tomorrow and get the ball rolling on the policy. At least you won't have any loans when you graduate."

"Okay. I'll see you Friday night. Love you, Mom."

"Love you, too. Stay safe, Emma."

We hang up, which brings me back to thinking about what to do next. Peter took out the life insurance policy when he found out I was pregnant. At the time, I thought it was a lot, but he said rule of thumb was seven to ten times your annual salary. Twenty years ago, two-hundred-fifty-thousand dollars sounded like a fortune, but in today's world—it's not. At least Emma won't be in debt; that's the most important thing. We always want our children to do better than we did. Hope and wish that they can go further in the world . . . make a difference. I'm proud my Emma is on the right track.

When I walk up to my house, my dog Rusty is sitting on the back of the couch with the blinds moved to the side. His face is plastered against the glass. He was a rescue and anyone that comes to my house is deathly afraid of him. He's a big clown, but Pit bulls have a stigma. When I get inside, he rolls onto his back and does his butt wiggle. He greets me every day like this. He's been my savior since Emma left for school.

"Hello to you too, Rusty. Did you miss me, big guy?" He waits, knowing what's coming next—the belly rub and then, most importantly, dinner. This is our daily routine. I wonder how he's going to react to Mitch tomorrow. Rusty can be very protective until he deems you safe, and then the big baby comes out in him. The rescue said that comes from him being used as a bait dog. Just the thought sends shivers up my spine. "Come on, big guy. I've got something special for you tonight." We head into the kitchen and I cook up a burger to add to his food tonight. After all, it's not every day I officially become a widow.

chapter
THREE

Mitch

I GET TO DOUG'S HOUSE TO FIND HIM SITTING ON THE porch, waiting for me. Our neighborhood is all duplex single-family homes. Each house has a one car garage. Some people turn their basement into a one-bedroom apartment. Usually they are not legal; too much paperwork and a lot of palms to grease to make it legal. There is a long flight of steps up to a porch, which is where Doug and I usually have a morning coffee or a beer. We have backyards but we basically use them for gardening. Sitting on the front porch together lets us keep an eye on the neighbor's comings and goings. Peter's neighborhood is very similar except his house is the end unit, so he is only attached on one side. We've been neighbors for twenty years. It was Doug, Peter, and me.

We were the three musketeers. Doug was the oldest by one year, so he always took control of everything. Twenty years. Twenty frigging years we've been waiting. Peter was supposed to come to my house that night before he went to the store for Amelia. The next day we were finally going to meet with the top jewel fence in the world. It took us a year and Peter jumping through a lot of hoops to even get the appointment. Peter was supposed to come to Doug's house that night with the jewels. We'd been sitting on them for three years, rotating the location. Each of us held on to them for a year. We were nearing the end of Peter's stint. We trusted each other with our lives, so why not trust each other with the jewels? But then Peter vanished without a trace. The crazy part of this whole thing is that no one even believed there was a heist. There was even a movie made about it. Of course, they got it all wrong. I mean, after all, there weren't any witnesses, so most of the story was made up. Even the Guinness Book of Records removed the heist from their book, stating there was no proof that it ever happened. Only the three musketeers— Peter , Doug, and I—knew the truth, but now we don't even have jewels to prove it! I slowly climb the steps, still lost in the past. When I get to the top, Doug is in his usual spot: sitting in a beat-up folding chair with his feet propped up on an old milk crate.

"Doug, were you afraid I wasn't coming back, either?"

He rolls his eyes, downs what's left of his beer, and pulls another one out of the cooler he keeps on the porch. "Asshole, I needed a break from that hag I'm married to. You're lucky, your wife left; mine just won't go away. Even now that my daughter is out of the house. What happened today?"

"Amelia officially became a widow today, and she agreed to go out for drinks with me tomorrow night. I'm going to push her to sell the house. And since I'm Peter's best friend, I will list it for her at a discounted rate. I mean, after all, she's a widow and needs every penny now."

"Wow, you really know how to spin the shit around. It does help that you're one of the top producing realtors in Brooklyn. Do you really think the jewels are in the house?"

"We looked everywhere we could think of. Peter's car was torched, and there was no body in it, so that was useless. Who knows, maybe it's in plain sight."

"So, what is your plan?"

"I'm going to convince her to let me list the house. I'm going to offer to do some of the changes and updating that needs to be done. I'll put her up in a hotel while I tear that place apart. Once we get the jewels, we will be on easy street." He crosses his arms and rests them on his ever-growing man-gut. He keeps up like this, he won't live to spend his portion.

"There's one big problem in your plan."

"What's that?"

"Peter. Do you really think he would have left Amelia seven months pregnant of his own free will? Come on, man. Why don't you be realistic?"

"There's a lot of what ifs, but we have to start some place. No, I don't think he would have willingly walked away. I think he was grabbed that night and who ever took him, killed him trying to get the jewels. I know Peter, he would never give up the location of the jewels."

"If that's the case, then why has no one bothered Amelia? I'm sorry, Mitch, I know you don't want to believe it—hell, all these years, I refused to believe it—but now, twenty years later, I'm starting to think Peter skipped with the jewels."

I take a few minutes to contemplate what he is saying. "Maybe they didn't know about her. He was supposed to be headed here with the jewels. Maybe he was on his way to pick them up. Or maybe you're right; maybe he had them with him and just skipped out of town, you know, skipped out on all the responsibilities of his life. Maybe he finally got that boat he was always dreaming about. It wouldn't take much to go down to Mill Basin, get on a boat, drive away and never look back. Hell, what do I know, do I look like a professional crook or a killer? Doug, we were three drunk college kids on spring break in Cannes. I know I'm grasping at straws, but what else did we have to look forward to?"

"Yeah, three kids who pulled off the greatest heist in history. The sad part is, we never saw a dime of it. The funny part is our kids are the same age we were at the time. Could you imagine them pulling off what we did?"

I can't help but laugh at the thought. "We are the three musketeers, each with a daughter. How ironic, but It's not like we could pass on the family business to them. Could you imagine trying to teach them to rob houses in broad daylight. One piece here and one piece there, all going unnoticed? When enough is accumulated, go out and sell it. It was the perfect way to build up our little war chest so we could get to France. I know our kids are clueless but in today's world, it's a whole different animal. Everyone is so worried about being politically correct. They could never do what we did, they wouldn't have the balls."

"Balls? You know we had to have big ones to rob that

place with machine guns filled with blanks. It helped that we had a few too many to drink at the time Peter came up with the plan."

"It's funny; whenever I think back to that trip, I always seem to remember a few more things, you know . . . little things. Sometimes it makes me wonder if any of it was real." He gets a somber look on his face.

"Mitch, when I think back, I remember Peter plying us with a lot of Tequila, and let's not forget the women that seemed to come out of the woodwork."

"Oh yeah, I almost forgot about the women. He hatched the plan that night. I still can't believe we never got caught. I mean, we walked into that hotel jewelry store in broad daylight with guns blazing. We took everything in sight and walked right out the front door."

"Don't forget the most important thing we took was the two black pouches of diamonds. I always wondered if Peter knew that they were being delivered the night before. Maybe that's why he insisted we needed to pull it off that morning."

"I think you're giving him way too much credit. I always thought he was just one lucky bastard."

"Do you ever wonder how much the jewels are worth today?"

I dig around in the cooler and pull out the last beer. "I looked it up once on the internet. In today's world, sixty million from 1996 would now be worth a hundred million. Although, we wouldn't have gotten that much from the fence. You know even if we find the stuff, we wouldn't get that much."

"Let's face it, Mitch, even if you find the jewels, we wouldn't know what to do with them. That was Peter's department, not ours. That was our set up from day one: you got the house listings, I was the repair man, and Peter would sell whatever we were able to lift from each house. Hell, you got your real estate license so you could sell houses when you were off from school. It was the perfect gig until Peter went missing."

"I know we stopped lifting stuff from houses because Peter was gone and we didn't know what to do with it, but maybe now we could figure out what to do with them. First and foremost—we need to find them. After that, we can figure out the rest. We watched Peter do it for years, surely we learned something from him." I look at my watch and realize in a few minutes my daughter will be calling. It's our weekly call and all I have left since the divorce. "I've got to go; I'll talk to you later." I toss my empty can into the trash and head into my house.

chapter
FOUR

Amelia

I SPENT MY FIRST NIGHT AS A WIDOW PACING THE FLOORS, trying to figure out my next move. Peter bought this house as a wedding present for me in 1999. How ironic that it's twenty years to the day and now I need to figure out what to do with it. I've spent some time looking the house up on a few of the internet home sites. My house is worth more since it's a corner semi-attached home. It has a one car garage and an illegal one-bedroom basement apartment. The rent from that apartment has helped me to pay the mortgage. Sadly, if I decide to sell it, I can't use that as a selling point.

I could talk to Mitch about the house tonight when we go for drinks. He has been in real estate for years, that's how Peter bought this house. He got it on a foreclosure, and it was a total gut job. Mitch, Doug, and Peter did all the work themselves. Hopefully that doesn't cause a problem for me. I think if Emma is okay with it, I'm going to sell it. The value has at least doubled since Peter purchased it. I could go and pay cash for a small place. The question is: where do I go? I need to make sure I'm going to fit in. After all, I've lived in Brooklyn my entire life. I've only left for vacations with Emma to Disney World. I know that I need four seasons and I need to be able to get to an airport quickly in case Emma needs me. That's really my only criteria other than wherever I go, it must be pet friendly. Where I go, Rusty goes.

I head into the kitchen for fresh coffee, taking stock of the rooms along the way. I never really changed anything, always hoping that Peter will walk through the door. I always thought he would come home with some wild story, but I think if he ever walked through the door now, I'd probably drop dead from a heart attack, or kill him. It's the not knowing that is the most frustrating part of all of this.

It's amazing how much you can get done once you have the death certificate. I went this morning and brought a copy to the insurance company, since they needed an original. I also contacted Social Security; they said I get two-hundred and fifty-five dollars to bury him. Yippie! I'm not entitled to survivor benefits until I'm able to collect Social Security. I'm only forty-two years old; by the time I'm eligible there probably won't be any Social Security. I thought of having a little memorial service for Peter, but who would I invite? The only people left that knew him are Mitch and Doug. It's not like they came around after he was gone. Hell, it's like everyone fell off the face of the earth. I thought about having it for Emma's sake, but she only has my memories that I shared with her. The more I think about it, the more I'd rather not have one. Hopefully, Emma won't bring it up. As a parent, you not only have to think about every step you take in life, you also have to keep in mind how everything you do affects your child. I always thought adulting would get easier as Emma got older. Boy was I wrong.

I saved up my paid time off so I could take a month off. It's not like I didn't know this day was coming. Hell, it's been looming for twenty frigging years. It just feels weird not going to work. I wonder if this is what it will feel like if I retire? I need to get this bullshit out of my head. I know I have to start my life now. Emma is an adult; Peter is legally dead. I can do whatever I want to. It sounds good. If only I could just convince my heart to follow my head. The constant ringing of the phone snaps me out of my pity party. It's my best friend Chloe Jones. She always seems to know when I need her.

"Hey, so how was it? I'm sorry I didn't call you yesterday, but you know my life is constant drama."

"Sadly, it was just like any other day, so you didn't miss much. Oh, you'll never guess who I ran into at the court house, Mitch Stein. What are the odds?"

"Say what?! No way that was a coincidence. You can't tell me you believe it was."

She's really going to go off the rails when she hears this one. "Well, not only did I run into him, but he asked me out for drinks," I inform her. She squeals and I have to pull the phone from my ear, or I'll go deaf.

"What did you say?"

"He's picking me up tonight at eight. Any advice?" I ask.

"Yeah, don't go. You know I don't trust him. Where has he been all these years? Not helping out his best friend's wife and kid, that's for sure. Fuck it, I know you're not going to listen to me, so make sure you wear something that shows off the girls. You know a girl has to work her assets."

I can always count on Chloe to keep it real. One night, many years ago, we had too much to drink and I let it slip that I always had feelings for him. At the time, she said nothing, but I'm sure she's filed it away for a rainy day. "I'm not interested in him that way." Lucky we're on the phone where she can't see me, or she would know I was lying.

"Oh, that's right, you have *The Beaver pleaser—AKA: The Beav—to* satisfy all your needs as long as your batteries don't die!"

"No need to worry about that anymore. I buy them by the case at Costco. I will never be left high and dry again." She's laughing, no doubt remembering the night I was banging on her back door because my batteries were dead, and the local corner store was closed for a funeral. "Desperate times, my friend."

"Call me when you get home. I won't sleep until I know what he wants and trust me—he wants something."

"I have nothing, so I don't know what he could want."

"The house; let's face it, he can make a pretty penny on it. I heard through the grapevine that his business wasn't doing so well."

"How do you know everything in my neighborhood when you don't even live here?!"

"People love to tell me their whole life story and everyone else's. I heard that's why his wife left him."

"You see, I only found that out yesterday. Why the hell didn't you tell me?"

"Because you don't need to be bothered with these people. They were Peter's friends and did nothing to help you when he vanished. You don't need any of them sniffing around."

I know she's right, but I still have to find out what he wants. "So, I gather you don't think I should list the house with him." She's quiet and I wonder what wheels are spinning in her head.

"On one side, he's hungry and will push to get it sold no matter what. On the other hand, I don't trust him. I've got to say no but go with your gut."

That really didn't help me at all. "I'll listen to what he has to say, and I'll let you know. Now I've got to get ready. Love you, kiddo."

"Yeah, yeah. Call me!"

Calls with Chloe are always fast and furious. She gets her point across and then she's gone.

chapter
FIVE

Amelia

AT EXACTLY EIGHT O'CLOCK, MY BELL RINGS. AT LEAST he didn't just beep the car horn, expecting me to go out. I've got my list of questions, and I'm nervous as hell. "Punctual," I say when I open the door.

"Of course. I built my business on being punctual."

His eyes do the "*I'm not looking but I really am slowly taking in every curve you've got to offer.*" I've got on the standard little black dress and, taking Chloe's advice, I made sure the focus is on my girls. The way he's looking at them, I might get him to sell my house for free. "Where are we going?"

"Hotel Delmano in the Williamsburg section of Brooklyn."

"A hotel, really? I don't know what you're thinking but . . ."
He holds up his hand and I stop in mid complaint.

"I'm stopping you right there. I picked it because they are known for their quiet rooms and I think that's what we need. The last thing I want is to be in a bar, having to yell all night. We haven't seen each other in years, so I would like to hear what you have to say."

Well I wasn't expecting that. "I'm sorry. It's just when you said hotel, I kind of freaked out."

"Amelia, trust me; you have nothing to worry about."

I hope not. I don't think I could deal with anything else.

It's wasn't that far away from my house. He quickly navigates us into the lounge area with ease. It makes me wonder how many times he's actually been here. I decide to order white wine so I can keep my clarity. He orders a dirty martini which would put me under the table. He also orders a few appetizers without looking at the menu. Now I *know* he's a regular.

"I guess you come here often."

"Enough. Like I said, it's a great place to do business. It's quiet and they don't let people stand around the bar. That keeps the noise level low."

"So, are you working me tonight?" I'm watching his body language. He adverts his eyes away from mine.

"Amelia, we are friends; I'm not working you. I was happy I ran into you yesterday and wanted to catch up, that's all."

"Mitch, that sounds all well and good, but where were you all these years?"

The waitress interrupts us with our food and drinks. He waits for her to leave, but I can see the cogs in is head spinning. I don't think he was prepared for my questions.

"I was raising my daughter, creating a business, and dealing with a wife that has a gambling addiction. I've had a lot on my plate. Now that my daughter is away at college and my wife is now my ex, I've found myself with more time on my hands. You know, the road goes both ways; you could have touched base with me. If you would have, you would know what a roller coaster my life has been."

Well, that stings. "You're right; I could have touched base with you, but I was working two jobs, trying to keep a roof over our heads."

He picks up his glass and holds it up to toast. "I guess we are both full of excuses. Here is to new beginnings."

We clink glasses and with my mouth being so dry, the cold wine is a welcome relief. "So, I do have some questions for you. When Peter bought the house, you and Doug did all the renovations yourself. If I decide to sell it, will I have a problem? I mean, I don't doubt what you guys did, I just want to make sure all the permits were issued, and everything is up to code."

"Like with any renovation that is over twenty years old, codes have changed. However, what we did at the time was up to code, so they would be grandfathered in. As far as the permits are concerned, we had everything that was required to get the certificate of occupancy. You won't have any problems. Are you considering selling it?"

"I've been kicking that can down the road. I'm not sure what's involved in it, or where I would go."

"Ahh, that's where I come in. Have you done any updates since Peter left?"

"You mean since he disappeared, no. I wanted to keep it

the same just in case he came back." He makes a tsking noise and shifts in his seat. Clearly, I've made him uncomfortable.

"Amelia, you've clearly decided to move on since you've legally declared him deceased."

"I did that so I can stop living my life in a holding pattern. Legally I can't do anything without that death certificate. His name is on everything, Mitch, including the mortgage and the deed. I had no choice but to hold on to everything. Even if I wanted to make any updates I couldn't, since that takes money. I worked two jobs for twenty years to keep that roof over our heads. After three months, I never heard from you or Doug again—his best friends. I know you said you were dealing with your personal life and your business, but what about Doug? He was the ringleader from when you guys were in grade school. You know . . . the three musketeers," I remind him. His eyes grow wide as he downs the rest of his martini.

"I can't speak for Doug, but let's put all that behind us; I couldn't be there then but I'm here now, and I'm not going anywhere."

"Okay, I'll at least listen to what you have to tell me." Our waitress comes by with another round of drinks and I can feel myself slowly relaxing. However, him telling me he's not going anywhere is not sitting well with me. I know when I replay this conversation for Chloe, she will basically loose her shit.

"I'll pull comps on the neighborhood and all the information on your house. Then I would like to come over, go over it all with you and see what we need to do to get you the most money out of the house. Does that work for you?"

"Yes, just give me a day's notice. Now, tell me what Brook has been up to." I try to divert the conversation away from me, so I'm no longer in the hot seat. Doug's daughter Vanni is the oldest, then Emma, and then Brook. Peter wanted our children to grow up together like the guys did, but that never came to be.

"Brook's great! You know how crazy the last year of college can be." His face lights up when he talks about her.

"What will she do when she graduates?"

"She's into journalism. Her dream is to be an analyst for one of the cable news stations. She did an internship in her junior year and after that, she was hooked. What about Emma?" he asks with as much enthusiasm.

"Emma will probably stay in Chicago after graduation next year. She loves it. Her major is Chemical Engineering and she is already being offered jobs from big pharma companies."

"Will you move to Chicago?"

"No. Someone once told me you can't follow your children. I really think that's true. What if I move there and then she meets someone that lives in New Hampshire? I need to find my own happy place. And, as long as I'm near an airport, I know I can get to her if she needs me."

"I never thought of it that way. I don't think I would follow my daughter. As much as I love her, I have a business here. Plus, I don't know where she will end up. Chances are it wouldn't be permeant. I'm too young to retire and nowadays you need millions to even do so."

"I'm getting ready to retire from the DMV. No, I don't have millions, but I've reached the max with my pay and retirement benefits, so staying will actually make it worse for me. I can still clean office buildings at night. Eventually, I would like to expand my little side business to something that could support me. Not in New York, though; I couldn't afford it."

"What kind of business?"

"It's an up-cycle business. I find junk, restore it and sell it. It started as a hobby. Sometimes it would help me during the lean months. The business grew so much that I turned my basement into my storage/showroom. Since I don't have a car, I turned my garage into my workshop," I add. His eyes grow wide as he twirls the olive in his martini. "Are you worried you have your work cut out for you?" I ask. He throws his head back and laughs. I can't help but laugh with him.

"You're good at reading me. Yeah, I'm worried. I'm sure I can handle it, though. The bigger question is—can you? If I start telling you to get rid of a lot of stuff, are you going to freak out on me?"

"No, I'll get a storage unit. I don't throw away much; I would rather find a use for it. My love of up-cycling came from having nothing and trying to survive."

"I wish I would have had the balls to be a better friend to you. In all honesty, it was awkward. My best friend walked out the door and never came back. It almost felt like a break-up. You know the fight over who gets to keep the friends?"

I think his remorse is real but after Chloe put her thoughts on him out in the open to me, I have doubts. "Well, let's put the past away and focus on selling my house."

"Deal. Now, let's get to know each other again. Tell me, Amelia, are you dating anyone?"

Well if *The Beav* counts, then I've had a steady date for the past twenty years. Well, minus the night *The Beav*'s batteries died, but I won't be sharing that with him. "I've had casual dates, however, until yesterday, I was still technically married. That really kept a lot of doors closed. Who knows what will happen now? What about you? How long have you and Becky been split up?"

"When my daughter left, so did my wife. It was for the best. Becky got hooked on fantasy football, which wasn't bad. But when football season was over, she discovered online poker. From there, she spiraled out of control. It was Brook that forced her to get help. I hope it sticks, but you know with any type of addiction there is always the possibility of slipping back. She put me in so much debt, I'm still trying to find my way out." For the first time since we got here, he slumps in his chair and his voice cracks. He gets a faraway look in his eyes, like a sadness that he can't break out of. The undercurrent of a strong wave that seems to be pulling him under.

I reach my hand across the table, taking his hand in mine and I give it a soft squeeze. "I'm so sorry, Mitch, that you had to go through all of that. You know, sometimes children follow their parents and by the time we realize it, they are already in trouble. Thankfully, Brook didn't go down the same path. You should be proud that your daughter had the strength to get Becky the help she needed."

At the mention of his ex-wife and her troubles, he signals the waitress for the check. "Amelia, it's getting late, and I have a closing in the morning. Will tomorrow around four work for you?"

When I glance at my watch, I realize he's right—we've been here for hours. "Yes, that would be great. Emma is coming home this weekend, so I can go over everything with her, including where I should move to."

As soon as he pays the bill, we head out. As we are walking to the car, he takes my hand. I'm startled but it feels comfortable. "Amelia, these cobblestones and your heels are a disaster in the making."

Well, okay then. So much for my thoughts on the hand holding. It's not because it feels good; he doesn't want the klutz to fall and sue him. I guess it's me and *The Beav* again tonight.

chapter
SIX

Mitch

WE ARE GETTING CLOSER TO HER HOUSE AND I'M feeling things I shouldn't feel. In reality, she is just another mark. At least, that's what Peter always called them, only . . . she is the wife of my dead best friend. I need to push aside whatever attraction I'm feeling for her; I'm sure it's nostalgia rearing its head. I need to keep my focus on the jewels. After all, that is the ultimate prize. When I pull into her driveway, I quickly get out and open the door for her. I want her to see chivalry is not dead. When I take her hand, I can feel it tremble at my touch. I wonder if I'm having the same effect on her that she is having on me.

"Thank you again, Amelia, for a wonderful evening. It felt good to unwind and catch up. I'll see you around four tomorrow." I lean in and kiss her on the cheek. I don't want to seem too presumptuous. She heads inside, closing the door behind her. Even if I wanted something to happen, she high-tailed it into the house so fast, I can still feel the wind from the door on my face. As I head down the stairs and into my car, I notice the upstairs light goes on. I vaguely remember the lay-out of the house. I wonder if that's her bedroom. Is she think-ing about me? Her silhouette appears through the curtains. I don't turn on the car lights; I just watch her. She begins to un-dress and as I reach to turn on my headlights, I wonder what kind of person it makes me, sitting here watching her like this. Her dress drops to the floor and my cock comes to life. With her back to the window she unhooks her bra, letting the straps slowly slide down. Damn she's good—really good—at this. It makes me wonder if she's done this before. Does she know that I'm watching? Is she putting on a show just for me, or am I delusional? Probably the latter. She steps out of view from the window and the light goes off. The party might be over, but my cock has a mind of his own. It's going to be an-other lonely night with just my hand for company.

Amelia

Oh, for heaven's sake; what the hell was I thinking? I slammed the door so fast that if he was an inch or two closer, it would have hit him in the face. When he moved in, I thought he was going to kiss me but at the last second, he shifted to the side and gave me a peck on the cheek. What the fuck was that about? Following my gut feeling that he's still in his car, I turn on the house surveillance and sure enough—he's just sitting in the driveway. Well, two can play this game! He wants to be a peeper; I'll give him a show. I race upstairs and within seconds I'm in front of the window with the blinds open. I make sure to slowly remove my clothes. When I get to my bra and panties, I turn around and give him the back view. After that, I hightail it out of the room, making sure *The Beav* comes with me. I head down the hall to the guest room, however, before I do anything, I've got to check in with Chloe before she calls cops. She can be a little crazy at times, but she is the one person I know that will always have my back.

"Hey, Chloe, I'm home safe."

"Okay, now tell me everything and don't leave anything out, because you know I'll find out." Somehow, she will; she always does.

I tell her about why his marriage failed, how he's trying to climb out of the debt from that. "It's sad. You know, you work your whole life trying to make an honest living and all it takes is one person to wipe you out. He talked about his daughter. He apologized for not being around more. He is coming over tomorrow to look at the house. He said he'll bring comps and let me know what updates I need to make it sell." I finish my report.

"What *aren't* you telling me?" she inquires. I look at *The Beav* on the bed and my stomach does a flip. What the hell was I thinking and what do I tell her? "Come on, girl, spill the beans! Did you do the nasty with him?"

"Geez, okay, I seriously thought about it! Odd thing is, when we were at the front door, he moved in for the goodnight kiss. I thought for sure he was going to try and take it to the next level. Instead, he kissed me on the cheek." Hopefully, I don't have to tell her the rest of it.

"So, he just left?"

"Damn it all to hell; how do you always get it out of me? I saw that he was in the driveway and he wasn't leaving so I put on a little show for him. There, that's it. I'm left alone frustrated and with you-know-who," I confess. Her laughter is contagious.

"Well, at least you have enough batteries to wipe that man right out of your thoughts!"

"Do you think the day will ever come when I can retire *The Beav?*"

"No! Never. I'm taking *Mr. Fuzz Buzzer* to the grave with me. You better be prepared to do the same. Okay, what time is he coming by?"

"Four. What time are you coming by?"

"Yeah, you know I won't leave you to your own devices. I'll be there at five-thirty. That will give you enough time to show him the house and a little extra in case he wants to do the nasty."

"Do you think he wants to?"

"Hell yeah! The bigger question is: what's stopping him? Look, I don't have to tell you that you were an easy mark to-night. Widow, horny, a few drinks—damn, I would have done you and I don't even bat for that team!"

"Maybe the fact that I was married to his best friend. Or maybe he just wasn't attracted to me."

"Girl, if he wasn't attracted to you then he's a fool. You've got killer curves in all the right places and we won't even talk about your Kardashian booty. Get some sleep. I'll try and get off of work early and come by. I'll let you know what I think when I see him in action."

"Alright, have a good night. I'll see you tomorrow." We hang up and now the thought of a workout with *The Beav* is doing nothing for me. I opt for curling up with Rusty and binging on Jack Ryan.

chapter
SEVEN

Mitch

I THOUGHT WITH SOME SLEEP THINGS WOULD LOOK clearer in the morning. Boy was I wrong. If anything, it only made things worse. I can't stop thinking about her. Not her house, not the jewels, not even Peter. Her and that body. Lord above, she's in her forties but has the body of a twenty-year old. I don't even know how that's possible. I know if Peter were alive today, he would be bragging like crazy. I need to get my mind off of her body and back on her house.

I pulled all the comps. Now it depends on what kind of updates are needed. I'm hoping enough to keep her away for a few days so I can tear the place apart. I think the jewels are still in the house. I know Doug doesn't think so but, if not, then where the hell could they be? I take my coffee and head out front. Every morning, weather permitting, I read my paper and have my coffee on the front porch. Doug usually walks over from his house and joins me. I head outside to find him already waiting.

"You actually beat me out here today," I mention as I study him. He looks like he's got a three-day old beard and bloodshot eyes.

"Yeah, I want to know what happened last night. Otherwise, you would be out here alone. Spill your guts, Mitch."

"I convinced her to let me look at the house and give her all the information on selling. Thing is, she's not one-hundred percent sure that she wants to sell it. You know, all the memories and shit. She gave me some shit that you and I weren't around for her and Emma over the years. She was right to call us out. I mean, after all, Peter was our best friend." I lightly smack the table with my paper before taking my seat. He rolls his eyes and sips his coffee.

"What if she decides she's not going to sell? Do you have a plan B?" he asks.

"No, do you?"

"You're single; you could fuck her into submission. Don't even try to tell me that you don't find her attractive. Any fool can see when you talk about her you get all fucked up in the head."

I nearly choke on my coffee. "What exactly does fucked up in the head look like?"

"Come on, man, it's a good plan B. Besides, when was the last time you got your rocks off without the use of your hand?"

"Some days I fucking hate you. I'll let you know what happens later." I gather my stuff and head inside. I hate it when he's right.

I must have rehearsed what I want to tell her all day. I have no idea why I'm so nervous. I've been doing this for over twenty years. I know the house like the back of my hand. I mean, I did all the renovations on it, so I know it's not that. It's her. She's stuck in my head. On top of that, the guilt is creeping in. If Peter was alive and our places were reversed, he would be doing the same thing, or at least I'd like to think so.

I pull up to her house and see she's outside in the garden, on her hands and knees, pulling weeds. My eyes instantly look at my cock, knowing he's going to spring into action. I keep willing him to stand down, only to realize I'm yelling out loud in my car. She sees me, gets up, grabs her water bottle and takes a swig. Watching her lips wrap around the bottle sends my mind in a tailspin. I've got to fuck this woman soon before I lose my ever-loving mind!

"Hey, Mitch, you're early," she says as I get out of my car.

I look at my watch and realize I am, by thirty minutes. "Yeah, my last appointment finished up early, and I thought I would just shoot over here. That gives me more time to look around. I hope you don't mind."

"No. I'll jump in the shower while you look ."

I follow her inside and as she heads up the steps, I find myself wanting to follow her upstairs and into the shower. She stops, turns around and smiles. "Why don't you start downstairs while I head into the shower."

I quickly snap out of it as her eyes glance down to my crotch. Right about now I'm in deep prayer, hoping my cock doesn't give me away. If I follow her eyes, I know I'm screwed. I feel a flush coming up my neck. Thankfully, she turns around and races up the steps. I head into the living room, which is like stepping back in time; everything is as it was the last time I was here when Peter was alive. I can hear the shower start, so I take the time to look for any hiding places that Peter might have had. I helped him with every aspect of this house. I try to think of anything that would be a clue as to where he could have hidden the jewels in the house. I can't think of anything. No loose floorboards. I lightly tap on the walls—solid . When I turn into the kitchen, I stop dead in my tracks. Coming through the doggie door is a beast of an animal. He's looking at me like I'm his next meal. I think he might be a Pitt Bull. He's covered in scars and patches of his hair is gone. What little hair he does have left is standing straight up like a bad mohawk. He's got a growl that is deep and scary. I think moving right now would be a bad decision, especially since his upper lip is beginning to curl up. I think I just might shit in my pants. That's when I hear her behind me.

"Rusty, no! Mitch, he's just showing you who is boss."

"I would say, at this moment in time, he is." She puts a dog biscuit in my hand.

"He can be bribed with biscuits. Show it to him." She nudges. I put it out in front of me and he slowly makes his way toward me. When his teeth are inches from the biscuit, he stops growling and gently takes it from me.

"I don't think I have ever held my breath that long in my life!"

"Once he gets to know you, he will be a big baby. I just wouldn't make any sudden moves until then."

"What happened to him?"

"He was a bait dog; I rescued him. Usually, if a dog is the runt of the litter and not a good fighter, they use them for bait. He looks a little ruff but he's my boy."

I slowly walk over to the kitchen table and pull out my paperwork. I want this to be somewhat legit. I make sure to keep one eye on Rusty at all times. "Why don't you give me a tour of the upstairs and then the basement?" She agrees and takes me around. I'm still amazed over how nothing has changed. When we get to the basement apartment, I'm in awe at some of the stuff she has restored. "You do amazing work, Amelia."

"Thank you. I've been selling a lot on eBay and now I have a store on Etsy. It started out of necessity, but I built it into a small business I love. The good thing is I can do it from anywhere."

"Have you thought any more as to where you would move to?"

"I was thinking North Carolina. I'm thinking that Emma and I can do a road trip on her next break."

"I've never been but I've heard nice things about it. As far as this house is concerned, some stuff needs to be modernized. There are also a few things that might have to be brought up to code. I want to call in a home inspector. Have him do a thorough inspection. After that, we can work off his list. Once I know what we need to do, I can put the costs into the sale price. How does that sound?" Before she can answer, Rusty runs past us, almost knocking me over as he races up the stairs.

"My friend Chloe must be here. Rusty has a thing for her."

She smiles. We follow Rusty. I have to say; I'm dreading this. I met her two times and both of them were not good. She has a way of making me feel like she has my balls in a vice grip. When we get upstairs, Chloe is on the floor giving Rusty a belly rub. No wonder he has a thing for her. She gets up and her eyes instantly lock on mine. For some reason, it's like she can see deep into my soul. Maybe it's just a guilty man talking.

"Hello, Mitch, have you figured out what you can get for the house?"

Something tells me she's going to be a problem. "Not yet, but I'll let Amelia explain it all to you. So, Chloe, how have you been? Are you still working as a 911 operator?" I try to take the spotlight off of me.

"If you would have been around more you would know that I'm an EMT in Williamsburg. You know, just sayin.'"

"Ouch. What can I say other than I'm sorry? I'm here now and willing to do whatever I can." This is me kissing ass, and I hate it.

"You say that now but let's see if you stick to it. I just came by to check on my friend and make sure she's not getting screwed again. On that note, I've got to get back to work; I'm pulling a double tonight. Amelia, walk me to my car, please." She smiles and follows Chloe out. I wanted to tell her that subtlety is not her forte, but I just shut up. No doubt I'm the topic of conversation. I head into the kitchen and gather my papers. I decide I want to wait before I do my sales pitch. Looking around, I venture to say a lot of work needs to be done. The bones of this house are good, which is why it held up so long.

Rusty leaps off the couch and runs to the door as Amelia

comes back in. "Sorry about that. She can be very protective of me. So, what have you decided?"

"Let's wait for the inspection report and we can decide after we see what needs to be done. It'll take about four hours. You don't need to be here, I will be. I will need a key, and you'll need to take Rusty out of the house while the inspector is here."

"Nothing against you, but I don't like anyone to have a key to my house. Can I let you in and then you can call me when you're done?" She's cautious and doesn't just jump right in. Her trust will have to be built.

"That will work. But when we list, I will need a key. You said Emma was coming home on Friday. I can get an inspector in here tomorrow. It will take twenty-four hours for him to email the report, which will work out great because then you can show it to Emma. Does that work for you?"

"Yeah, but how are you able to get someone in here so quickly?"

"I've been in this business over twenty years; I've got connections and if need be, I can call in a favor or two. Now I need to get going. I want to get started on this."

"Okay, I'll walk you out."

I get in my car and head home. Hopefully Doug is still somewhat sober and can help me get an inspector on short notice.

chapter
EIGHT

Amelia

WELL THAT WAS NOTHING LIKE I WAS EXPECTING. He never talked money. He didn't show me any comps and to top that off, Rusty didn't like him. Maybe I should just forget the whole thing. Damn it, Peter, even after all these years, you're still fucking with me. I have an uneasy feeling about having anyone in the house when I'm not here. I think I wouldn't mind if I could leave Rusty here, but I understand that I can't. I didn't tell Mitch that I have a surveillance system and if he saw it, he never questioned me about it. Since Peter has been declared legally dead, I'm second-guessing every decision and I have no idea why.

Me: Hey I know you're working, but tomorrow the home inspector has to come. They need Rusty out of the

house. And Mitch said he could handle the inspection for me, so I don't need to be here, either. I didn't say anything about the surveillance system. Should I?

Chloe: What happened to your smarts? Of course, you don't say anything. If they find it and ask you about it, just play dumb. Look, I told you there is more to him sniffing around you, now that Peter is dead, then meets the eye. Get your head out of your ass and pay attention!

Me: Okay, calm down. I was just double checking. Have a good shift and be safe. I'll let you know what happens.

Thank God I have Chloe to always snap be back to reality.

Mitch

When I pull up to my house, I find Doug sitting in his usual spot on his porch. Thankfully, he seems sober, probably because his wife Dedra is away for a few days. I don't know why he stays with her. I swear it's a misery-loves-company thing with them. "Hey, I've got a lot to go over with you. I did a quick search around her house and I didn't see anything. It's kind of creepy, almost like time stood still. I also noticed a home surveillance system, so I needed to be careful. Anyway, I need a home inspector for tomorrow. Tell me you can pull this off, please."

"You're lucky I've got a partnership in a home inspection company. I can get it done. Now, tell me what happened today."

"She has a pit bull that is scary as shit. She did nothing in the home, no updates at all. Oh, and remember Chloe Jones? Well, she's Amelia's best friend."

"That's not good news; Chloe is a bitch. She could fill her head with reasons not to sell. Do you think she's set on selling the house?"

"No, she doesn't have any idea where she would even go. On the plus side, she has a small business that she runs out of her home. I'm not sure if it's legal, chances are it's not since she was renting out the basement to help pay the mortgage, and that's not a legal two-family. She made sure to mention that to me, no doubt to make me feel bad about not being around to help her," I add. When he's nervous and deep in thought he strokes his beard. Right now, he's practically pulling it out.

"So, if she doesn't want to sell, your big plan is to report her to the IRS for an illegal business? Come on, man, you've got to come up with something better."

"I don't see you contributing any big solutions."

"I could make the inspection report come back all clear, you know just a few minor things. That would help her get a better price than the house is worth. You know, sweeten the pot, so to speak."

"Or you could make it come back a total fucking disaster. Then I sweep in like the white knight and offer to take it off her hands. She can get out without any repercussions, which is better than your idea."

He gets up and begins pacing on his tiny porch. "What makes yours better?"

"New York law says a seller can be held responsible for repairs after the closing if any of the facts about the house were withheld."

"I know that, but she can't be sued if she didn't know," he counters.

"Right, but it is the responsibility of her lawyer at closing to inform her that she can be held responsible. On top of that, the inspection company can be sued. Since ignorance is not a defense, you'd be setting yourself up for a lawsuit."

He sits back down and pulls a beer out of the cooler. "That's why I have insurance."

"Why don't we wait and see what the report has to say? We can decide what to do after that," I suggest. He stares at his beer for longer than usual which can only mean the wheels in his head are spinning.

"Okay, but what are you going to do about the surveillance system?"

"I'm going to pretend I didn't notice and let the inspector do his thing."

"Or you could disable it."

I head over to the cooler and pull out a cold one, even though it's early for me. "No, I'm not going to do that. We've been lucky that no one ever caught on that we were robbing them when they sold their houses. I've just stepped back into her life after twenty years, add her friend Chloe into the mix, and I don't want to rock the boat."

"Look, Mitch, I get it, but we haven't stolen anything in a very long time, years in fact. It just became too risky without Peter. Even with Becky gambling away all your money, we still stayed clean. It's not like anyone would suspect us. I have a guy that could disable it in a New York minute. Hell, Sid works for Con Edison—I could have him cut the power to the whole neighborhood. That would give you all the time in the world to look around."

It doesn't take me less than a minute to realize it's a bad

plan. "Doug, you are involving too many people and that will come back to bite us in the ass. We've lived for the past twenty-plus years without the jewels, I think we can wait a little bit longer. Besides, what's the rush?"

"I'm not getting any younger. Besides that, I think it would be my ticket out of here."

Bam, there it is. "Do you really think if we found them and were successful at fencing them that you would be able to leave this life behind? Why don't you wake up and smell the shit you're trying to shovel? The odds, my friend, are not in our favor. Besides, Amelia has been fucked over big time, so let's try and do this without fucking her again."

"There's the operative word: Fuck. You want to fuck her, hell you wanted to fuck her when Peter first brought her around. So, answer this one, Mitch, why have you waited all these years? Was it because you were a married man, remaining faithful to a wife who thought nothing about stealing from you?"

"Fuck you; I'm done here. Text me the time for the inspection tomorrow." I crush my can and toss it in the trash before heading into the house.

chapter
NINE

Mitch

I HATE IT WHEN DOUG IS RIGHT. WHEN PETER STARTED bringing Amelia around, it was more like a friendship between them. He knew I had a thing for her but was too shy to do anything about it. Then one day, he announced he was going to ask her to marry him. I felt like it was a sucker punch to the gut. I tried to talk him out of it, but it only made him mad. I think he went after her because he knew how I felt, but at that point, what could I say? I could never be that guy that would break up someone's happily ever after. By the time I met Becky, Peter announced that Amelia was pregnant, and I knew that the door was permanently closed. Right after that, I asked Becky to marry me. I know I settled. Hell, everyone but Becky knew I settled. However, I loved

Becky, just in a different way. She gave me the best gift in the world: my daughter, Brook. I took my vows seriously and had no intention of ever walking away. It was Becky that walked out on me. Now I'm trying to deceive the one person that I really did love. In this game of deception, I'm in too deep to do anything about it now.

Doug: Everything is set for tomorrow at 11 am. I thought about everything and for now, we will do it your way.

Me: Thank you.

I quickly shoot a text over to Amelia letting her know what time I'll be there. She said when I get there, she'll give me the key and head to the dog park with Rusty.

Doug wasn't too happy when he found out about Chloe. Him and Chloe are the same age and went to public school together. Peter and I went to Catholic school. We knew her from around the neighborhood, but we were too young to fit into her crowd of friends. The only reason Doug bothered with us is because we lived in the same apartment building. I wonder what he knows about her that we don't. Maybe I need to research her past. If nothing else, I can make sure that nothing from her past can get in my way. Geez, now I'm sounding like a paranoid asshole. I shrug it off and call Brook.

"Hey, Daddy, what's going on? Two calls in one week. Come on, Dad, you can tell me the truth, did you meet someone?" She giggles and it makes me smile.

"No, did you?" I laugh but she gets really quiet. "Oh my gosh, Brook, did you really meet someone?"

"Yes. I didn't say anything sooner because I didn't want to

jinx it. We've been dating for six weeks. He's a year older than me. His major is meteorology."

"Does this guy have a name?"

"Benjamin."

"So, when do I get to meet Ben?" Right now, my insides are twisted and I'm ready to hurl. She's too young for any of this. Well, in my mind, she'll always be to young.

"He goes by Benjamin, and I'm not ready for the whole meet-the-dad thing."

"Does your mom know about him?" Again, silence.

"Here's the thing, Mom came up here for a surprise visit last weekend, so she met him already."

"Are you kidding me?! Brook, how did that happen? I mean, I know it was a surprise visit and all, but you didn't have to bring her around him without me." Great, now I sound like a jealous idiot.

"About that . . . it just so happens that was the weekend that Benjamin was moving into my place. And before you get all crazy, Dad, it was my idea. I want to test the water before I make any permanent commitment."

Test the fucking water, what the hell? I'm conservative and raised my daughter the same way. Testing the water is not in my wheelhouse and I didn't think it was in hers.

"Dad, are you still there?"

"I'm just surprised, Brook. I didn't raise you to be a *test-the-water* kind of girl."

"Look, Dad, I didn't want to have this conversation over the phone, but here goes nothing. I don't want to end up like you and Mom. If I get married, I want to make sure it's perma-nent. You and Mom were just functioning through marriage. I never heard you tell Mom you loved her. I never saw Mom light up when you entered the room. I don't blame either of you, but I don't want to end up like you. I know this hurts you, which is something I never wanted. I'm sorry, Dad, but I need to find my own way. A way that will work for me, and Benjamin moving in works for me."

I mute the phone and pace around the room, yelling and cursing. I'm looking for something to punch. I want to blame anyone and everyone. I catch a glimpse of myself in the hallway mirror. I stop and fight the urge to punch it. Instead, I curse myself. The one person I never wanted to hurt is the one person I really did.

"Daddy, are you there?"

I unmute the phone. "Yeah, I'm here. Brook, you're the one person I never wanted to hurt. Everything I did in life I did for you. I'm sorry if I wasn't a fairytale father. I was doing my best, I still am."

"I don't blame you, really I don't. I don't know everything between you and Mom. I only know what you both chose for me to see. Honestly, I really don't want to know. It's water under your bridge, not mine. What I do know is that I want something more than that. You always told me not to settle and, Daddy, this is me not settling."

"Well, at least I did something right. Is he good to you? Does he make you laugh? You know, at the end of the day, looks will fade but if you can still laugh then you've got something worth holding on to."

"So far, he does all of that and more. I promise I will introduce you to him soon."

"Okay, I'll let you go."

"Wait, Dad, you never said why you were calling?"

"Nothing important, sweetie, sometimes I just need to hear your voice."

"Okay, I love you, Dad, and I'll talk to you soon."

"Love you, too."

I hang up and now I'm left second-guessing everything I ever did in the name of my daughter's happiness and well-being. What kind of father am I that I couldn't see what I was teaching her? Not by words but by my actions. It's really true—*actions speak louder than words*. I never did tell Becky out loud that I loved her. I didn't hate her. I did love her in my own way. I believe there are so many ways to love a person. I loved her for giving me my daughter. I loved her for making a home for us. I loved her for all the things she tried to do. I just wasn't in love with her. I was in love with Amelia. It was an unrequited love. I never told her out of respect for my friend. I wonder if I told her today what would happen. No, no, no, I'm not going down that road. I promised myself I would never go down that road. And I always keep my promises. My focus is the jewels and only the jewels.

Brook

"How did he take it?" Benjamin asks me. He knew I was worried about telling my dad. He wanted to tell him and Mom together, but he doesn't know them, and I wanted no part of that.

"Better than I thought he would. Although, I think I

might surprise him, make this weekend a long one and head home."

"I can't get off of work this weekend or I would go with you."

"That's okay. I think we could use some one on one time. You know, so he doesn't feel like he's being pushed out of my life."

"Okay, then when you get back, we have to work out when you are going to meet my parents."

I roll my eyes. From everything he's told me, it should be a piece of cake. It's my dad who can be a pain the ass. "You're on."

chapter
TEN

Amelia

IT'S ELEVEN AM AND, LIKE CLOCKWORK, MITCH PULLS UP with the inspector right behind him. Rusty is curling his top lip and not in a good way. "Rusty, stop it," I command as the gentlemen make their way to my door. "I'm sorry, Mitch, I'm sure once he gets to know you, things will be better. How long do I need to stay away?"

"It will probably take four hours or so. I will text you when he's done."

"Great. The doors unlocked. I'll see you later."

I head down the street practically dragging Rusty with me. He keeps turning his head around and growling. Maybe he knows something I don't. I quickly wipe that thought from my head as we head to Rusty's favorite dog park. It's not near the house but it's an off-leash park. As long as he's vaccinated and has his license with him then he's good to go have fun. I made sure to put on one of his t-shirts to cover his scars. He can be scary looking without it. When we finally get to the park, I unleash him, and he takes off. He is so fast that sometimes it's hard for me to keep my eyes on him. He usually does this for about ten minutes. After that, he sits by my side and watches for anything that interests him. Usually it's a bird; squirrels are boring for him. When I look at the time, I see it's already been an hour. It's lunch time, but before we hit the hotdog cart, I'll see if Chloe wants to join us.

"Hey, I'm at the park with Rusty. Do you want to have lunch with us?"

"Hot dog Dan?"

"Of course, you know I have an addiction to hot dogs."

"I swear I have no idea how you can stay so thin when you eat them practically every day. Wait for me, I'll be there in ten." She hangs up. Rusty sees a bird and takes off. I think he believes he can fly. He stops chasing the bird and takes off running full speed. I turn to see where he's headed, and Chloe comes into view carrying lunch. I don't know what he loves more, Dan dogs or Chloe.

"I swear his obsession with Dan Dogs came from you." She sits down and passes Rusty his dog. He doesn't take it and doesn't move.

"What the hell, Rusty, eat your damn dog."

I look at it and begin to laugh. "He has to have ketchup and mustard. No worries I'll give him mine." I pass him my dog, and he finishes it in three bites.

"I swear, Amelia, I don't who's stranger—you or the damn dog. What happened when Mitch showed up today?"

"Other than Rusty curling his upper lip and letting out a low growl, nothing."

"So, why the hell did you call me out here on my day off?"

"I'm attracted to him. There, I said it out loud and I can't take it back. Is that a bad thing?"

"Wait, you're attracted to Mitch?"

"Yeah, and I thought about it last night. I have to admit that I was first attracted to him when I met him, way back when." Her mouth is hanging open and I want to stick my hot dog in it.

"Attracted enough to retire *The Beav?*"

"Yeah, that kind of attracted."

"Wow, that's big. But why didn't you act on it when you first met him?"

"Because of Peter. It was like a whirlwind with him. Before I knew it, we were engaged. Plus, you know it was the whole best friend thing."

"My beef with him is why the hell is he coming around now? You can roll your eyes all you want, but I'm telling you there is more to this. What do you have that he wants?"

"Maybe because he was married before. Now, he's not and neither am I. Do you think I should take a shot?" I give Rusty some water and then sit back next to Chloe.

"No matter how much I protest, you're going to do whatever you want anyway. Maybe put it out there and see what he does. I wouldn't be chasing him; no man is worth that."

I know she is right, but sometimes knowing what is right and doing the right thing is totally different. "I've been alone so long that I feel like there is an invisible wall that no one will penetrate."

"No one will penetrate it because you won't let them. If you really think there is still something there that you left behind all those years ago, then maybe you need to open the door. Look, when Peter left, it did a number on your self-esteem. Twenty years is a long time and you've got to try and get past that. Even if it is with Mitch."

"Don't you think I've tried?! I know twenty years is a long time, Chloe, I'm the one living it. I think if I just knew what happened to him, I could move forward with my life. I need closure."

"Maybe if you let Mitch get closer you might find some sort of closure to move on."

"What about the house, do you think I should sell it?"

"If you do, where will you go?"

I put Rusty's leash back on and he quickly jumps up. "Come on, Chloe, let's head toward the house. I don't know where to move. I have you here and my part-time job at night cleaning offices. I need to move someplace more affordable."

"I can understand that. I'm living paycheck to paycheck. A lot of people are moving to Florida since there is no state tax."

"No, not going to happen. Florida is an annex of New York. I was thinking North Carolina. I did some research and I could take the proceeds from the house and buy something for cash. I would also have to buy a car in order to get around. If I keep it simple, I should be able to do this. Providing I get a good price for the house."

"Okay, when we get back to the house, show me what you came up with. I promise I will keep an open mind."

As Rusty leads us towards home, I'm trying not to get too excited about moving. If the house needs a lot of repairs, I won't be able to do it.

chapter
ELEVEN

Mitch

DAVID, THE INSPECTOR, LET ME KNOW HE'S ALMOST done here, so I sent Amelia a text to start heading back. I walk him to his truck, out of surveillance range. "David, I know I have to wait for the official report, but how bad is it?"

"Considering nothing has been touched for twenty-plus years, it's not that bad. There are a few updates that will be needed but, all in all, I would say you can get it done for about two or three thousand dollars."

"Thank you, David. Email me your bill with your report." He leaves and I head back inside to wait for Amelia. I can't help myself; I know the camera is watching but I slowly walk around, trying to remember what each room looked like when Peter first got it. I remember the house was in foreclosure, and he picked it up for a song. It was really trashed. The neighborhood was in a downturn, not like today with the gentrification of the different areas in Brooklyn. I thought he was nuts, but he saw something none of us did. He saw the future of what Brooklyn could become. Now these houses that have had nothing done to them are selling for a minimum of six-hundred thousand dollars. She only owes fifty-thousand dollars, so she could walk away with a nice chunk of change here. I try to not think like a realtor as I walk through the house. I need to think like Peter, like a thief. If I was Peter, where would I have hidden them? When I head upstairs, I stop in the doorway of Amelia's room. I stare at the iron bed and I get a twitching in my cock. I can only imagine how unbelievably fantastic it would be to have her in that bed. Every inch of her at my disposal. Lost in my own desires, I didn't hear the front door, that is until I hear that distinct growl. I slowly turn around and Rusty is staring at me with that curled lip. Amelia and Chloe are behind him with a look on their face like *you just got busted.* I try to ignore the obvious and focus on the house. "Hello, ladies. Rusty, my ass is not a prime cut of meat, thank you. The inspector just left. Did you have fun at the park?" I ask. Chloe pulls Rusty back and he finally calms down.

"Was there something wrong with my bedroom that I should be aware of?"

Everything would be right if we were in that bed together. "Not that I know of. I was just making sure everything was locked up before I head out."

"When do you think we will have the report back?"

"Either tonight or tomorrow at the latest. I need to get to

my next appointment. I'll touch base with you later." I quickly hightail it out of there. Rusty hates me and Chloe is suspicious of me, so, at this point, less is more.

Amelia

"Well, do you still get that feeling when it comes to Mitch? Could it be you're remembering who he was then and not the man he is today?"

"Maybe, but I think I want to try and get reacquainted with the man. Figure out who he is today. I don't want to base it on who I remember from my past. You know as time goes on the bad things fade away. The only thing remaining are the good memories. Does that make sense?"

"Yeah, it's kind of like you can't move where you vacation."

I cock my head and look at her like she's nuts, which some days she really is. "What the hell are you talking about?"

"You know the good and bad thing. Anyway, I've got stuff to do. Do you need me for anything?"

"Nope. Go; I've got this. As soon as I get the report, I'll let you know what it says." I shoo her on. She gives Rusty his usual back scratch and heads out the door.

I hope Mitch can get the report early enough to explain everything to me before Emma gets home. I know she'll have so many questions. I only hope I have the answers. In the meantime, I need to research some more places to live. I've lived in Brooklyn my whole life. The thought of moving out is overwhelming but the thought of staying is just as stressful. If I sell the house and decide I want to say in New York, I couldn't afford to buy anything. However, if I sell the house and move out of state, I could afford a lot more. Then there are capital gains. I looked it up, and we are talking thousands of dollars. My head is beginning to pound. I close the laptop and head into the kitchen for some wine. It's been that kind of day.

Mitch

I hightailed it out of there. I don't feel comfortable around Chloe. Maybe I should find out her past from Doug, that way I wouldn't feel so intimidated. I just feel like she's looking right through me. Like she knows what I'm feeling, what I felt all those years ago. How is that even possible since I don't understand what I'm feeling or even why.

When I round the corner, I see Doug sitting outside with his daughter Vanni and my daughter Brook. *She never said she was coming home this weekend.* I quickly park in my driveway and head up the steps to Doug's porch. Brook throws her arms around my neck like she always did as a little girl. Maybe dealing with Amelia is making me nostalgic or maybe the fact that Brook is in a serious relationship is doing it. When she finally let's go, I pull back, squeeze her shoulders, and look into her eyes. "Everything okay?" Her eyes have always given away her secrets.

"Yes, Dad. I missed you, that's all. I just got here and found Vanni outside with Uncle Doug. We were catching up. Everything okay with you?"

I smile and pull her into another hug, happy that I'm able to. "Yes, everything is great. Vanni, how is school?"

"Good. I came home to celebrate. I was offered a job when I graduate this year. It's a really good position with The Veteran's Association. I'm going to revamp their entire computer system. I'd bore you with all the details. Basically, it will eventually make the veteran's life easier and hold the government more accountable."

"That's fantastic. I'm very proud of you." Vanni has always been the one out there that is going to right all the wrongs in the world, which is really funny, considering who her father is: the most negative, conspiracy theory guy I know. I'm surprised she came home this weekend, with her mother out of town. Then again, maybe she didn't know. "How about we all go out to Bella Gioia for dinner to celebrate? Vanni, I'm sure you can't find true New York pizza in Dallas, Texas."

"Nothing even close! Oh, don't get me wrong, Uncle Mitch, they try, but I swear there's something in the water here that can't be duplicated anywhere else."

"Okay, then Bella Gioia it is." Doug heads down the steps and quickly tosses his beer can in the trash before getting into my car. He knows he's been drinking and would never get behind the wheel. The rest of us climb into the car and head out, just like old times.

chapter
TWELVE

Amelia

How do I get reacquainted with Mitch? I mean, I'm not about to call him to come and help me like all of the sudden I'm some sort of damsel in distress. Besides, I've survived all these years on my own, so he would see right through it. Sometimes I think back to when we first met and how possessive Peter would act around him, like a dog lifting his leg to mark his territory. Is that what Peter was doing?

It was Mitch and Peter's last year of college. Doug graduated the year before, but he never gave up on his friends. Peter brought me into the group as a friend, nothing more. Everyone in the group became inseparable. Mitch and I started to hang out together more and more. Then, all of a sudden, Peter decided to take our friendship to the next level. I was young, and it was surprising to say the least. Before I knew it, I was saying *I do*. Within a year after that, Peter was gone and I was pregnant. What a crazy rollercoaster my life has been. I was dumped at four into foster care and then left alone and pregnant. At least I did better than my birth mother. I held on to my daughter and put her needs before my own. I learned what real responsibility is. Emma and me . . . we did okay, and we will be okay. I head into the kitchen to put up a pot of tea and in walks Emma.

"I'm so happy to see you. I thought you were coming in tomorrow?"

"I only had one class tomorrow and it was canceled, so I decided to head out early." I look at her with skepticism but decide to let it go.

"I was just putting up the tea kettle, do you want a cup?"

"Sure, then you can tell me about the house and moving." She heads into the living room while I put up the tea kettle. I head in and curl up on the couch next to her.

"Mom, what's going on, you seem off."

"Not really, it's just that these decisions are life-altering. I'm too old to make a mistake."

"Really?! You're not that old. Maybe it's the fact that you're making major changes. Big changes can be very scary, especially when you're the type of person who follows a routine their whole life."

"Have I really been that kind of person?" I furrow my brow, thinking about it. She cocks her head to the side and bites her bottom lip, which is something her father did whenever he was trying not to laugh at me.

"Mom, you've lived in the same house for over twenty

years. You've never done anything to update the place, not even a new coat of paint. You've been at the same job since Dad left. Hell, you've been there so long that they are forcing you out. Now you are thinking of selling your security blanket and going someplace where you know no one."

Her words sting. I know she doesn't mean them to sound so harsh, but they do. The kettle begins to whistle. I jump up and quickly head into the kitchen, trying to hold back my tears. I fix the tea and before I head back into the living room, I wipe away a tear that has finally escaped. I curl back on the couch and hand hers to her "Truth is, I haven't decided what I'm going to do. I heard that you should move someplace where you have at least one friend. Like you said, I've lived my life in my little bubble, but I have to start somewhere. I'm just not sure where that somewhere is."

"Let's start with the house. Have you found out what it's worth in today's market and what you need to do to get it sold? I would think a paint job, at least."

"I'm supposed to find out everything tomorrow since the inspector came today. Mitch is going to go over everything with me. I'm sure some repairs will need to be made."

"Okay, no sense trying to figure out the house until we have all the facts, so let's put that part of the equation aside for now. Where will you go? When you are looking for places to live, what are you looking for?"

"Well, I don't know anyone outside of New York, but I know I can't stay here, it's so damn expensive. I looked into Florida, since I saw on the news that a lot of people are moving there. The economy is cheaper and there is no state income tax. However, I remember from our trips to Disney that I don't like the weather. I was thinking North Carolina or Tennessee. Four seasons but more tempered. Tennessee has no state income tax, but I'm leaning towards North Carolina. Plus, I read that southern people are very friendly and welcoming."

"Don't you think you should visit before you decide?"

"Well, of course I plan on it, and Chloe will be coming with me, so you needn't worry. Now, why don't you tell me what's bothering you?"

"It's hard to put into words. The thought of you selling this house, the only home I've ever known, will be gone to me forever."

"I told you I wouldn't sell it if it bothered you. I can call Mitch and tell him to forget the whole thing." I reach for my cell phone, and she stops me.

"That's not what I want you to do. I know the best thing is to sell. I just need to come to grips with it all. Plus, I worry about you. Why don't you take an apartment near me in Chicago? Give yourself a chance to research everything before you buy."

"That would mean I'd move twice. I made myself a promise that when I got out of foster care, I would put down roots and never move."

"Well, you can honestly say you keep your promises!" We both laugh, and it feels good.

"Mom, tell me about Mitch. You never spoke about Dad's friends. What's he like? Does he talk to you about Dad much?"

"It was weird, at first, seeing him after all these years. We made a deal that the past is behind us. I don't want to look back, Emma; it's not healthy. Besides, I had to grieve twice for the same man. The day he left and the day I declared him legally dead. I spent a whole day notifying all the agencies and getting his name off every single thing. It's amazing how much work it is. The insurance company issued the check so that should be here soon. When that comes, you can wipe out your student loans. The total is two-hundred-fifty thousand dollars. Will that cover everything?" Her eyes open wide, registering her shock.

"Cover everything and then some. I'll probably be able to buy my own place. It's overwhelming to me that someone I've never met will be taking me to the next level in life."

"You are a part of him. I'm grateful, and I look at it like a gift from heaven."

"Do you think I can meet Mitch?"

"Actually, you will be meeting him tomorrow. In the meantime, I think we should call it a night. We will have a full day come the morning." I give her a hug and watch her head up to bed with Rusty following closely behind.

chapter
THIRTEEN

Mitch

IT'S VERY EARLY. I HEAD INTO THE KITCHEN AND GRAB A cup of coffee. I don't want to wake her, so I head outside to read my morning paper. The sun has just come up and it's going to be another beautiful day in New York City. I was happy that Brook and Vanni were able to catch up last night. I'm no fool; I know Brook came home this weekend to sooth the blow from the other night. The way she looked when she was talking about Benjamin told me all I needed to know— she's in it with him for the long haul. I'm lost in my daydream until my vibrating phone dances across the café table. It's a text from Amelia.

Amelia: Good morning. Emma came home early, so she will be here when you come over.

Me: I look forward to meeting her. I just checked my email and the report came in. I haven't looked at it yet. What time would you like to get together?"

Amelia: How about eleven-ish.

Me: Okay, see you then.

Amelia: Be forewarned; she's probably going to ask you a lot of questions.

Me: I'll be ready for them.

I've never seen Emma, not even after she was born. I couldn't bring myself to go visit. When Amelia went into labor, none of Peter's friends were there to help her, me included. I think, for me, it was guilt. I don't know why Doug stayed away. To this day, we've never spoken about it. For him, it was always about the jewels, nothing more. For me, I was a married man who was in love with another man's wife. I loved my wife, but I was in love with Peter's wife. I knew seeing her pregnant and alone would be the hardest test I would ever face as a husband. It would test my faith and I knew I would fail, so I decided the best thing—no—the safest thing I could do for me and for her was to stay away. It doesn't mean I did nothing for them. When I heard Amelia was interviewing at the DMV, I called a friend and made sure she got the job. If it ever got to the point where she would lose her house or there was any danger for Emma, I would have come forward. I honestly believed she would meet someone and move on. I didn't know what it took to get someone declared dead and how that could hinder her moving on.

I wonder what questions Emma will have for me. Hopefully, I can answer them without making her father look bad. Maybe I should bring Brook with me. She is around

Emma's age, and it would be a good ice breaker. I'm about to get a fresh cup of coffee when Brook comes out with two cups.

"Dad, did you even sleep last night?" I help her with the coffees as she sits next to me.

"Yes, but it was a broken sleep. So, tell me more about Benjamin."

"What do you want to know?" Well, I guess this will be like pulling teeth.

"Let's start with the basics, you know . . . how you met. Tell me about his family. That kind of stuff." She's staring into her coffee like it's a magic eight ball.

"I tripped in the cafeteria and fell flat on my ass. My tray flew up in the air and landed in my lap as my books skidded across the room. I was covered in mac and cheese, along with my cup of coffee. All of the while, trying to break my fall. Even though there were a lot of people in the cafeteria, he was the only one who came over to help me. That showed me what kind of person he is. He helped me up and cleaned up the mess. He even replaced my dinner. As far as his family, he is the oldest. He has a younger sister that thinks he walks on water. He grew up in Jacksonville, Florida. You've heard of food trucks; well, his parents own a food boat called Diamond Reef. They take their boat out to different areas that are very popular, drop anchor so other boats come by to buy lunch."

"Wow, that's very inventive. How did he end up in Boston?"

"He was given a scholarship for his first year and then after that, his parents paid the rest so he wouldn't have any student loans. He's very grateful to them for that, just like I am to you for paying my way. So many of my friends are in such debt when they graduate that they will never see the light of day."

"I'm happy to be able to do that for you. I guess now might be a good time to ask you for a small favor. I don't know if you remember me mentioning an old friend of mine, Peter Mach. Well, he passed away, and it looks like I'm going to be selling his house. I have an appointment today with Amelia, Peter's widow, to go over the home inspection report. Her daughter Emma is in town from college. I was wondering if you would come along with me and maybe offer some moral support to Emma?" I didn't tell her it took twenty years to declare him dead. That's Amelia's business.

"Of course. What time do we have to leave?"

"It's not that far; around 10:30 will work. After that, we can do whatever you want."

"Sounds great. Now how about we talk about you dating? You can't sit around here every night commiserating with Uncle Doug."

I pick up the New York Post and begin flipping the pages until she pulls the paper right out of my hands. "Maybe, Brook, I'm just not ready to put myself out there. I know you don't think I loved your mom, but in my own way I did. We have a past and maybe I'm not ready to put it away."

"Dad, you know she's dating, right?"

Another sucker punch in my gut. "No, I didn't, but I can't say I'm surprised. Your mother was never one to let the grass grow under her feet."

"Well, somebody had to do something, so I made you a profile on The Over Fifty Crowd. It's a new dating website for people your age."

I think my chin just hit the ground. "You did what!? Have you lost your mind? Why would you do that without asking me first?"

"If I asked you first, you would sit here and hem and haw over the whole thing."

"I know you're right, but I just don't think I'm ready. Can you please take it down or at least deactivate it?" She gets up, presses the newspaper into my chest before heading inside. As she walks away, I hear her mumble something to the effect that I'm a stubborn fool. Nice to know what your daughter really thinks about you. Hopefully, she cools off soon.

Me: Hey, just wanted to let you know that I'm bringing Brook with me. I thought she would be good moral support for Emma.

Amelia: That would be great. See you soon!

chapter
FOURTEEN

Amelia

I'M HAPPY THAT HE'S BRINGING BROOK. IT WILL BE nice to meet her and put a face to the name. Plus, she will be a good distraction for Emma. Chloe worked another double, so I'm sure she's out for the count. If I don't keep her updated on everything, there will be no living with her.

Me: Hey, I wanted to leave a message for you. Mitch is coming over today with his daughter Brook. Emma came in a day early. I'll let you know what the house is worth and what needs to be done.

Chloe: Hey, I just got up for a cup of coffee. Glad Emma is there for you. On another note, guess who has a profile on The Over Fifty Crowd. Yep, it's our friend

Mitch. When you get a minute, check it out. I found it to be very interesting. Call me later.

Oh my gosh, I can't believe he's on there. So many times, I was tempted, but then my nerves got the better of me. Should I pull up his profile or mind my own business? Oh, fuck that; I need to see what it says. I quickly fire up my tablet and go on to the site. After saying no to every pop up under the sun, I finally get a one-week free trial. I put in Mitch Stein and up pops his picture. I'm not sure when it was taken, but he looks happy. It lists his likes and his stats. Then there is a small bio. It just doesn't seem like him. Out of the corner of my eye I see Emma coming down the steps. I quickly close my tablet. The last thing she needs to see is me on a dating site, checking out Mitch's profile.

"Good morning, Mitch will be here soon. He's bringing his daughter, Brook. She's around your age and thought you might like someone to hang out with. I hope you don't mind, I've wanted to meet her, so this was a good opportunity."

"So, what you're really saying is, you're as nosy and heck and you want to use me as an excuse." She laughs, so hopefully she lets me off the hook.

"I'm curious; you said you were friends with him before dad vanished, so why did I never meet him or any of Dad's friends?"

"That's a question you'll have to save for Mitch." There's a knock on the door. Speak of the devil; Mitch is here.

As I let them in, I'm taken back on how tall Brook is. Her legs seem endless. She has beautiful chestnut hair and eyes that match. "Come in, please." I quickly make the introductions.

"So, Emma, your mom said you have some questions for me. I'm all ears, so ask away," Mitch says.

"Mitch, what can you tell me about my father, and please don't paint him as a larger-than-life superhero." At first, I thought maybe having Brook here would make Emma shy about asking him questions about her father, but it doesn't seem to bother her.

"I see you take after your mom. Well, Emma, your dad and I grew up together. We both went to Catholic school. He graduated from college but had no idea what to do with his life. With my help, he bought this house. We renovated it, and your dad was really good at it. He talked about flipping houses for a living. He was a man ahead of his time. His other great love was being on the ocean. As kids, we hung around the marina, him more than me. He was always taking odd jobs just to go out on anyone's boat. One summer, he got us both jobs as deckhands on a yacht. After that, his dream was to have his own yacht. Unfortunately, that never came to be."

"If you were such good friends, why didn't you come around after he left? If it were me, I would have checked on our family a lot over the years."

Wow, she just went right for the jugular. I lean in a little more; even I want to hear this one.

"I think I was in denial that my best friend was gone. I never knew anyone that just up and disappeared without a trace. And honestly, I was a little scared. I was young and stupid. I didn't know what to say to your mom without feeling awkward. As time continued to march on, it became easier to just stay away."

"Do you have any idea why he disappeared? I mean, you have to admit it's very odd."

I suddenly realize I was holding my breath, anticipating his answer.

"It is very odd. Like everyone else, I have no idea. I'm sorry. I wish I had more answers for you."

"I guess I have to forgive you. Besides, it's not healthy to carry a grudge after all of these years," Emma says with a sigh.

"Do you have any other questions for me?"

"No, my job here is done. Now why don't you get those comps out and we can go over everything."

I watch Mitch and notice once he gets nervous, the tops of his ears turn bright reds. "Of course. I made copies for both of you. If you notice, I found three houses that sold or are up for sale. They closely match this house, with the exception being they are renovated and yours isn't. I would say with the minor fixes that came up in the inspection report, you can walk away with six-hundred-fifty thousand dollars. It shouldn't take me long to sell it since the market is hot right now. I'm able to cut the fee down, so instead of you paying a total of six percent I can knock it down to four percent."

"How much will my mom have to pay for the repairs?"

"Around two or three grand max. But Amelia, you have to figure out where you want to live before you do anything else."

I'm staring at him like he has three heads while I try to quickly do some mental math. "How much am I going to have to pay in capital gains?"

"You'll need to sit down with your accountant. There are deductions he can take to get it down. I know since you lived in the house two years or more it knocks two-hundred-fifty thousand dollars off of the sale. There is a formula that your accountant will use. Depending upon where you decide to go, you could pay for a house in cash. You have a lot of options, but you don't have to decide today. You and Emma should enjoy the weekend, discuss all your options, and we will talk more about it on Monday. First and foremost, you need decide where you want to go."

"I had no idea this house was worth that kind of money. You're right, I really need to make my decision as to where I'm going first. I'm leaning towards Asheville, North Carolina. I've been researching it, and it seems to have everything I'm looking for. Chloe offered to go with me to check it out."

"Mom, who knows, maybe you'll end up on an episode of House Hunters." She's laughing and Brook joins in.

"Oh, and if you decide to sell, you might want to start thinking about downsizing. While the inspector was here, I went room by room and made a list of some of the stuff you will need to purge." He starts flipping through his papers until he finds his list and passes it to me.

"Holy Hanna, it's three pages long!"

"I warned you ahead of time. Buyers don't want to see your stuff; they want to visualize their stuff in the space." He's packing up his things, but I'm fixated on his list.

"Okay, ladies, Brook and I are going to head out. Emma, it was very nice to meet you. Enjoy your weekend at home." He gets up to leave as Brook and Emma exchange numbers. They also make plans to meet up later for coffee. I'm glad he brought her with him. Emma has her friends, but this is a connection to her father, no matter how distant it may be.

chapter
FIFTEEN

Mitch

As Brook and I head home, my mind wanders back to that summer on the yacht. We had the time of our lives. We were young, fit, and tan. Needless to say, for us, it was a summer of love or, at least, that's what Peter called it. That was also the summer that Peter discovered older, married women, many of them.

"Dad, are you listening to anything I have to say?" I realize Brook has been talking to me.

"Honestly, no. I was lost in my memories."

"I've never seen you like this."

"Like what? This is me doing my job."

"No, you're very melancholy. I said I thought you handled Emma's questions about her father very well. You hardly ever talked about him. I didn't know you were that close."

"When my dad moved us into the projects, Peter was the only one who would talk to me. Back then, the world was very racially divided. Different nationalities mixing together was frowned upon. Neighborhoods were actually divided by nationalities. You never ventured out of your neighborhood. The world is nothing like it is today. In some ways, the world was better back then."

"How so? I would think, as a whole, we are more tolerant now."

"Just the opposite; we are less tolerant now. I think the internet changed the world forever. The internet is a double-edged sword. On one hand, it opened the world beyond our little neighborhood. On the other hand, it lets bad people into our living rooms. Sometimes they're in the form of bullies or pedophiles and sometimes they create scams to steal from those who don't expect it. Like I said: double-edged sword." Look at me calling the kettle black.

"I can understand your feelings, even if I don't agree with you. So, back to Peter; how did he die?"

"He went out to get Amelia something when she was seven months pregnant and never came back. No one knows what happened to him. Amelia had to wait twenty years to finally declare him legally dead. That was last week. Emma never knew her father, only the stories her mother told her."

"But you only met Emma today, how is that possible if he was your best friend?"

I take a deep breath and slowly exhale. "It's complicated, at best. I'm here for Amelia and Emma now and that's what matters most."

"Really? How complicated could it be? I think about all the things you and I did together and, poor Emma, she had no one." I didn't think it was possible, but I feel even worse now.

"Can we change the subject, please? I'm trying to do the right thing now. That should count for something, shouldn't it?" She keeps staring at me like she's trying to dissect me or something.

"Oh, my God, Dad, I don't know why I didn't notice this sooner; the way you looked at Amelia—you had a thing for her, that's why you stayed away. Tell me the truth, Dad. I told you, that I never saw Mom light up when you entered the room, and the same goes for you. Yet, the way you look at Amelia is different."

"I'd like to change the subject now. What are you doing for the rest of the day?"

"I'll let you out of the hot seat for now. I invited Emma to go for drinks with Vanni and me tonight. Was Uncle Doug friends with Peter?"

"Yes, but not as close as I was. Uncle Doug marches to his own drummer. I think it's nice that you're including Emma." The three musketeers live on . . . how ironic.

Brook and Vanni left to pick up Emma, and I finally have the house to myself again. What a crazy day. First, I get interrogated by Emma, which I was expecting. Then, my own daughter decides to give me the third degree. That I wasn't expecting. I wish I wasn't in so deep with the hunt for the jewels. I have a bad feeling that this is not going to end well for any of us. I have an idea I want to run by Doug. It's still early enough, so I head next door. He never locks his door; I let myself in and can hear the television blasting.

"Hey, Doug, I wanted to run something past you. Now that the kids are gone, I figured we could talk in private." We head into the living room and he shuts off the television.

"Yeah, I was hoping to talk to you about Amelia's house. Did you get a chance to look around?"

"Well, yes and no. I was limited to what I could do because of her surveillance system. I didn't want to look like I was snooping or possibly doing something nefarious. I really don't think the jewels are hidden in the house."

"Why?"

"Nothing in the house was touched since the day Peter left. It's actually kind of creepy."

"Look, Mitch, they have to be somewhere."

"What about telling Amelia everything. We could give her Peter's cut. Lord knows there's more than enough." He's stroking his beard, which he usually does when he's deep in thought.

"What if she goes to the police? She could be one of those goodie two-shoes."

"Doug, do you really think they would believe her? They didn't when she reported Peter missing. Now she's going to try and convince the police that he was part of an international crime ring?"

"Yeah, a ring that consisted of three guys on spring break. You're right; no one would believe her. Let's wait till the kids leave. Now tell me about the house. How much are the repairs going to cost, and do you think we should just buy it outright?"

"I don't think the repairs are going to be high. I think we could bring it up to code and make any other repairs for five grand. That would include making the basement apartment legal."

"Do you want to rent it or flip it?"

"I think we should rent it. We would have a nice monthly income."

"Okay, after the kids leave. Now tell me about Amelia; do you still have a thing for her?"

"I put that to rest twenty years ago. Let's just focus on the house. I've got to go. I'll talk to you tomorrow." I get up and head out, leaving him no time for a rebuttal. If I don't, he won't give up and I'm not prepared to go down that road with him.

chapter
SIXTEEN

Brook

"EMMA, THANK YOU FOR COMING OUT WITH US tonight. I can't believe our parents were friends for so long and we never met. So, tell us about yourself." She's fidgeting and seems nervous. I want her to feel comfortable with us. I don't know the whole story that my dad skirted around today. I do know my dad, though, and, for some reason, he's acting like a guilty man.

"Nothing much to tell. I had a normal childhood. I'm majoring in chemical engineering. I love dogs, country music, and live for my morning coffee. That's about it. Now tell me about you guys."

Vanni and I give her the express version of our lives. It's all pretty basic except, of course, I now have a steady boyfriend.

"Vanni and I made my dad a profile page on The Over Fifty Crowd dating app. We should make one for your mom. Did you notice the way they looked at each other? The pheromones in that room today were off the charts crazy."

"I didn't notice because I was focusing on the information your dad had about mine. It might be good to make the profile."

I pull my iPad out of my tote and fire it up. "No time like the present to get the ball rolling. Emma, did your mom say anything to you about her past?" I know I'm fishing but something with my dad is so off.

"No, she doesn't like to talk about it. Over the years, when I would bring up my dad to try and find out more information, she would seem so sad. After a while, I just stopped asking. What about you, has your dad said anything?"

"No, which is all the more reason I need to get to the bottom of this." I pull up the website and begin the search. "Okay, I'm in now, let's start building a profile for your mom." It feels very strange to do this. She gives me enough information to build the profile. While she searches her phone for a picture, I write the bio. Finally, I'm done, and I pass Emma the iPad.

"What do you guys think?" I ask. Vanni pulls her chair closer to Emma, so she can see over her shoulder.

"Emma, do you think your mom will get upset with you about this?" Vanni has a point. I'm close with my dad; I know how far I can push him. I don't know Emma's relationship with her mom.

"I think it's great. I also think my mom's best friend, Chloe, will find it before my mom ever will. If nothing else, Chloe and Mom will have a good laugh about it."

"There's a feature on the site to poke someone you're interested in and send a hello. I'll go back to my dad's profile and poke your mom." A few clicks and I'm done.

"Okay, now we wait. I hate waiting."

"Brook, I don't think I've ever met anyone that likes to wait. Does your dad even know about this profile?"

"Yeah, he wasn't happy about it."

"Let's just forget about the whole matchmaking thing. So, tell me about your boyfriend. Is it serious?" This must be what it feels like to be in the hot seat. It actually makes me squirm a little.

"We just moved in together, so yeah, it's becoming serious enough. I've dated in the past, but I never had the butterflies in the pit of my stomach feeling until I met Benjamin. He's met my mom but not my dad. I told him over the phone the other day that we are living together and that my mom already met him. That's why I came home this weekend; I wanted to make sure he was okay with everything." Even though this is personal, I'm very comfortable with her.

"Is he?"

"No. He might look happy on the outside, but I'm sure on the inside he's flipping out. He's conservative in his thoughts about women. It's probably his Catholic school upbringing."

"Did you also go to Catholic school?"

"Yes. I went to Mary Queen of Heaven through the eighth grade. After that, I put my foot down and demanded I go to public high school with everyone else in the neighborhood. Vanni is a year older than me, and she went to the public school. My parents finally gave in, letting me go as long as Vanni promised to look after me. What about you, Emma?"

"I went to public school. It wasn't bad. There were a lot of kids in my neighborhood, so we all watched out for each other."

"At least you didn't have to grow up with a fear of Nuns. To this day, I shake when they enter a room!"

"Are you both only children?" Vanni turns towards her and takes the lead.

"Yes, our parents always said, 'one and done.' I'm sure we gave them a run for the money." Our laughter fills the room. Emma seems to get a faraway look on her face right before she gets up.

"Well, ladies, I've got to get going. I'm only in town for a short amount of time and I promised my best friend I'd pop in for a visit. Thank you for including me today. I'll let you know if my mom says anything about the profile." She's grabbing her purse and pushing the strap up her arm before pushing her chair in. She waves as she heads out the door. Something tells me that going forward, we are going to see a lot more of Emma.

Emma

I catch an Uber to head back home. I know I could have asked them to drive me, but I didn't want to interrupt their evening. Besides, the more I think about the profile, the more I think it was a bad idea. I agree with Brook that there was something there, but I don't think it's any of our business. I've seen my mom have some casual dates in the past, but she never seemed too enthusiastic about any of them. Maybe there was a reason, one that I'm not privy to. I get home to find all the lights are on. No doubt she's waiting up for me. I open the door, and she's not around.

"Hello, anyone home!" I shout out as I go room to room. Finally, my mom comes up from the basement. "There you are. I was worried when you didn't answer me."

"Where could I possibly have gone? I got an order for a piece, so I was in the basement working on it since it was too cold in the garage. Did you have a good time? Brook seems nice, what about Vanni?"

"I had a good time. They were both very nice. I need to talk to you about something."

"Oh boy, am I in trouble?"

"No, I am. Brook made up a profile for her dad on one of those dating sites for older people. We also made one for you."

"Why would you do that? Do I seem desperate or something?"

"No, it's just that Brook felt there was something between you and her dad, you know, sparks or some shit like that. I thought maybe you could use a little push, so I went along with it. Afterwards, I realized I was wrong, but I didn't know how to get out of it. Your life, your business—not mine. I'm sorry."

"First of all, I knew about his profile from Chloe. Does Mitch even know he has a profile on there?"

"He does, and apparently, he wasn't too happy about it. I will take it down, if you want." She walks into the kitchen and puts up the kettle. When she's deep in thought or upset, she puts up tea. Me—I grab the Ben and Jerry's.

"Let's see what happens if you leave it up. If it gets too weird, I'll have you take it down. Now, tell me what else happened tonight."

"It was strange. Not bad . . . just different. I grew up not too far from them and, yet, we are very different. Our fathers were best friends, but I could never see us as best friends. I know that sounds strange. You brought me up making do with whatever we had. I don't need some designer's name all over my handbag. I guess I choose function over fashion." The tea kettle whistles, and she fixes them with a shot of brandy, or as my mom always refers to it, as the poor man's cognac. She brings the cups in and curls up on the couch across from me.

"I think I raised you to utilize whatever you had. Rely on no one but yourself. But most of all, adjust your own damn crown."

"Were you really happy with Daddy? I mean, were you with him because of me or were you really in love with him?" These are the questions I've never felt ready to ask because I wasn't ready for the answers. Suddenly, I think I am.

"I met your dad and he introduced me to his friends. We all hung out together. I think I was closest to Mitch. It's also how I met Chloe. She was dating Doug on and off. One day she got pissed and told him to fuck off. She walked out and never came back. Till this day, I don't know the whole story. I figured if she wanted me to know, she would tell me. Anyway, I always enjoyed Mitch's company and I think he enjoyed mine. We seemed to be getting closer and then, out of the blue, your father started showing up everywhere I went. We got closer, and Mitch backed away. Then one day, your father asked me to marry him. Since I grew up in foster care, I had no family.

His family had passed away. So, we got married at city hall. A month later, I was pregnant with you. I loved your father, and I'm grateful to him for giving me you. Since Mitch came back into my life, I have questioned some things but, at the end of the day, you can't go back; time waits for no one. He moved on and so did I. Truthfully, I'm not sure if I would start anything with him. Too much baggage. Chloe always says everyone has baggage but make sure it's only a carry on. Does that answer your questions?"

"Yes, I think maybe you should dip your toe in that pond and see what happens. After all, you never want to go through life wondering what could have been."

We finish our tea. I'm so tired, I think it's time for me to go to bed. "I'm going to turn in. I'll see you in the morning. Love you, Mom."

"Sweet dreams. Love you, too."

chapter
SEVENTEEN

Mitch

I T'S ANOTHER NIGHT OF PACING THE FLOORS, WONDERING what I should do. The more I think about telling Amelia everything, the more I think, on so many levels, that it's a bad idea. I know if she went to the police, they wouldn't believe her—that's not even my main concern. I just think it would ruin any shot I have at getting to know the woman she is now and not relying on the memories from all those years ago. A shot at being a part of her life again. I wish the past was not going to bite me in the ass. If only there were another way around this. Maybe I should tell her how I really feel. How I've felt all these years: I loved her, and I never stopped. Not only did I never tell Amelia how I really felt, I never had the balls to admit it to myself. To own it like a man. Now that I'm at a point in my life where I could take things to the next level, I fear it's too late. Maybe the best thing for all of us is to help her sell the house so she can move away. Why is everything so difficult? Maybe it's become more difficult with age. It was so easy back in the day to throw together a plan. When you're young, you don't dwell too long on the consequences. It seemed like it only took Peter minutes to put together the plan for the heist. Hell, it took us longer to figure out how to get the money for the trip than the actual heist. Thinking back, I really believe Peter started to formulate the plan during the summer of love. That summer changed all our lives. I have to remind myself to forget the past and stay focused on the present. I grab another cup of coffee and fire up my laptop. Time to check in on this website and make sure Brook took down my profile. Low and behold it's still there and on top of that, someone poked me and left a message. I should just get Brook's sorry ass down here now to delete the whole thing, however, my curiosity is getting the better of me. I open it and it's a simple hello from Amelia! That's not so simple . . . How the hell did she find this? She must think I'm looking for a hook-up. Oh, wow, why is she on here? She's beautiful; she doesn't need this. It can't be safe.

"Good morning, Daddy, I see you found your profile. Oh, and look, Amelia has one too. What are the odds?"

"Exactly, what are the odds? You might as well tell me what you did. I'll find out sooner or later."

"I know you will. Emma helped Vanni and me make a profile for Amelia. Honestly Dad, it was written all over your face yesterday that you care about her. Maybe this will be the push you need to finally do something to help yourself. Emma thought maybe it was the push that her mom needed, too. In the meantime, just deal with it. Now, on to another subject. When do you want to come up to school and meet Benjamin? I thought long and hard about it and I think I'm ready for that to happen."

"First of all, does Amelia know about this?"

"Probably. Emma seems really close with her mom, so I venture to say that she's told her by now. What's secondly?" She smiles and cocks her head to the side. She knows she's got me.

"Why the turn around on Benjamin? The other day you were hiding him and everything about him from me. Now you want me to meet him. What changed?"

"I did. After meeting Emma, I realized I'm lucky to have a dad that's still part of my life. I want that to continue for a long time. Whomever I end up with needs to get along with you and vice versa. It's a joint effort."

"You're becoming wiser with age."

"Dad, I'm not fifty for Pete's sake."

"Okay, point taken. As soon as I get everything settled with Amelia's house, I will come up and meet Benjamin. Happy?"

"Immensely." She throws her arms around my neck and I nearly fall out of my chair. My baby girl is not a baby anymore.

I gave Amelia the entire weekend to digest everything and to figure out where she wants to live. Tomorrow evening, when she gets home from work, I'll head over to see what she decided. In the meantime, I want to talk to Doug again. He's going to think I'm nuts. Maybe I should tell him the truth—that is—if he hasn't figured it out already. Today is trash pickup day; I can hear him putting his garbage pail out to the curb. I head out to catch him before he goes back inside.

"Hey, Doug, come in here for a minute. I want to go over some stuff with you before tomorrow." He nods and makes his way over to my steps, huffing and puffing while walking up them. I wish he would quit smoking and drinking, but that's beating a dead horse.

"Don't tell me—you changed your mind again. Am I right?"

"Yeah, you're right; I did. Look, I think telling her everything is a bad idea. I think we should just buy the house using our holding company. This way she will have no idea who the buyer is. After she moves away, we flip it, but not before looking for the jewels." The more I think about it, the more I think it's a great idea.

"This is all because you never got over your hots for Amelia. You can close your mouth now. I knew about it for a very long time. I'm just surprised when Becky walked out that you didn't go running to Amelia."

"Was I that obvious?"

"From day one. Honestly, I think that's why Peter married her. He was jealous of you. He always felt that you got the best of everything, that he always came up second. That's why he was so thrilled that summer when you both worked on the yacht where he was in charge of the entire crew, and that meant you too." I'm trying to let what he's saying sink in.

"How could I have been so blind to all of this?"

"Look, Mitch, you're my best friend, but you always see the good in people. You want to help those who can't help themselves. If you weren't so conservative, you would make a great bleeding-heart liberal." He laughs, but I don't see anything funny about this.

"What if we do all of this and there are no jewels? What's our next move?" I ask.

"If we come up empty handed then we should just call it a day. The whereabouts of the jewels died that night with Peter." He shrugs.

"Are you prepared to do that? I mean, we took the chance of a lifetime and won. Are you ready to walk away?"

"Yes, we won, but we lost too. They say hindsight is twenty-twenty and, in this case, it's true. We should have put the jewels in a safety deposit box. That way they would have been safe, and it would take the three of us to get access to the box. We shouldn't have trusted Peter as much as we did. When he planned the heist, we thought he was crazy. After we actually pulled it off, we thought he was a genius. See what being young and stupid got us? We made a stupid mistake that costs us big time. I think going through every inch of the house is the end. Do we have a deal?"

"Yeah, we do. I'm ready to get on with my life."

"So, does that mean you're going to get your balls out of your ass and try to have a relationship with Amelia? I mean it's only been twenty-somewhat years."

"How could I have anything with her knowing I have a big secret that involves her husband?" I throw my hands up in disgust.

"Here's what I think you should do. Let's do the house

deal. Afterwards, if we don't find anything, you go to her and tell her the truth. Chances are she won't believe you and she got top dollar for her house."

"And if we find the jewels, then what?"

"That's easy; you tell her the truth and give her Peter's share of the bounty." He makes it sound so easy.

"What if she goes to the cops? What if she doesn't believe me? What if she hates me?"

"That's a lot of *what ifs*. Look, you won't have a clue until it happens. Just follow the program."

"Well, I don't really have a choice. I guess we are buying her house," I blurt out in a strained voice. He gets up and whacks my shoulder in agreeance before heading out the door. I'm left sitting here, wondering how the chips are going to fall.

chapter
EIGHTEEN

Mitch

AS I HEAD TO AMELIA'S HOUSE, MY HEART IS IN MY throat. Aside from the big heist, everything else we stole to make that trip possible was just pennyante shit. Besides, it was in my younger days. I'd like to think I've turned my life around. I'm a much different man now, and what do I have to show for it?—nothing, I pull up just as she's walking up the street. She's beautiful. Her chestnut hair bounces with every step she takes. I was such a fool, a fool for her. I should have spoken up twenty years ago. She sees me, smiles and waves. With my heart in my throat, I get out of the car and meet her by the steps.

"Mitch, I'm so glad you came by early; there's something I want to talk to you about. Let's head inside, please." My mind should be on my job, instead, it's on the sway of her ass.

"Have a seat at the kitchen table while I put up the kettle." She sets everything up, and I'm taken back that she remembers my love for earl grey tea.

"I can't believe you remembered my favorite tea."

"A good life is made up of a million little things, things that make us feel loved and special. It's never been about the big stuff with me."

"Thank you for being who you are. Now, what did you need to talk to me about?"

"Our children were up to no good. It seems they made us each a profile on a dating site. They even had me poke you and say hello. I just wanted to let you know it wasn't me. I will have Emma take it down."

"I found out about it probably around the same time you did. Although, would it be so bad if it was true?" She blushes and I feel bad I put her on the spot. Maybe I'm assuming too much, or is it hoping?

"So much time has passed that we really don't know each other; we only remember the past. Sometimes, when I look back, I forget the bad stuff. It's like a fade-to-black sex scene in a good book."

I nearly choke on my tea. "Not exactly the answer I was expecting, but I get it. Let's just take one day at a time. In the meantime, have you come to any conclusions as to what you want to do about the house?"

"I did. I spent the weekend going over everything with Emma. I've decided I would like to sell the house and move to Asheville, North Carolina. There's just one thing I want to do before I do it. I want to make a trip to Asheville, and I would like for you to go with me." Again, I nearly choke on my tea.

"Why do you want me to go? I would think you would take Emma with you. I mean, I don't mind, just surprised, that's all."

"You are a professional, so I would like your help on purchasing a home. I've researched the area and pulled up some stuff I found interesting. I have a lot of vacation time before I retire, so that wouldn't be a problem for me."

It's not what I was expecting. I'm trying not to act excited, but the thought of going away with her to the mountains is making my cock spring to life, yet again. "I would be honored to help you through the next step in your life. I suggest we get the work on the house done this week. After that, we can go and find you something suitable. I have a feeling once we list this house, it will sell right away," I surmise. She has a huge smile and it's beautiful.

"That sounds great. I'll email you over the houses that I found, and I'll make a reservation for us at the bed and breakfast in town. Is this weekend good for you?"

"Yes, that sounds great. So, tell me how you settled on Asheville?"

"You're going to laugh but I first saw it on an episode of House Hunters. When I started researching it, I found it's an artsy type of town. Plus, I think Rusty is going to love living in the country."

"Okay, today I'm going to line up the workers to get started. I'm going to need a key."

She's swirling her spoon in her tea, never raising her eyes toward me. "I only have one key."

"I can take you to the hardware store to get another key made. It will be safe, I promise you. Plus, let's not forget about Rusty. He will put the fear of God into anyone that tries to come through the door."

"Okay, this is a big step for me. I'm putting my trust in you, which is not something that comes easy for me," she says. I have to try to remember she's been alone all her life with only herself to answer to.

"I get it. We can take this slow, but once the house goes up for sale, you will have strangers coming in here. On top of that, you can't keep Rusty here while there are people coming in and out. I'm surprised your insurance company didn't give you a hard time about him. So many insurance companies are putting on breed restrictions."

"They don't know about him. Since no one's complained, I didn't think I had to notify them."

"Well, all the more, we will keep him out of the house when anyone is coming. I'll put in the listing there is a dog, that you need an hour's notice. If need be, I can take him to my house while people are here." Her smile is huge. I know if I want to get on her good side, I can focus on Rusty. I pull the contracts from my attaché and pull my chair closer to hers.

"Let's go over the contract and then we can go to the hardware store."

"Sounds great. Do you want to stay for dinner? We can grab a pizza on the way home."

"There's always room for pizza and cookies!"

We finish up the contracts and head to the store. Before I know it, it's eleven o'clock at night and we've eaten half the pizza, and a whole bottle of red wine. A half of pizza doesn't sound like much but when they are New York slices, it's a big deal.

"Mitch, can I ask you something?"

"Of course, Amelia, I'm pretty much an open book." Except for the fact that I pulled of the heist of the century with your husband whose been missing for twenty years along with the jewels.

"What do you think really happened to Peter?"

"What do you mean by *really?*" I ask quickly. She shifts in her seat, seemingly uncomfortable.

"I don't believe that he just vanished in the middle of the night. I would like to think he didn't just walk away from his life with me. I mean, after all, I was seven months pregnant, and that would just suck in so many ways."

"I agree; it would suck, but it wouldn't be anything new. Unfortunately, plenty of men take the easy way out—women, too."

"You didn't."

"I'm not like plenty of men."

"Is that why you stayed with your wife?" she asks, then quickly gasps. "I'm sorry; that just flew out of my mouth. It's really none of my business." Her face turns beet red before she turns away from me.

"Amelia, look at me, please." I reach out and slowly stroke her cheek until she turns back toward me. "There are a lot of reasons I stayed with Becky, some of which I'm learning were not for the best, as I thought. You know Peter and I went to Catholic school together. We were taught to love, honor, and respect our spouses until death. Honestly, I was not in love with my wife and she really wasn't in love with me. We married each other for all the wrong reasons. When we had Brook right away, I knew

I would never leave. I didn't want her to grow up in a broken home. What I didn't realize is that Becky and I were just going through the motions, and Brook was very aware of it. Last week she told me that she was having her boyfriend move in so they can *test the waters*. She didn't want to end up like her mom and me. At first, I was hurt but then, I took the time and thought about it. She only knows what I showed her: two parents coasting through life. That's not what life should be about."

"That's so sad. Why did you settle?"

This is my opportunity to put it out there, but I'm not ready to tell her how I feel. "I settled because the one person I truly loved was with someone else. I would never come between them, so I walked away."

"Wow, if you had it to do all over again, would you do anything different?"

"Of course, I would want to but if I did, I wouldn't have my daughter; she is my world."

A calming look comes over her face and her whole body seems to relax. "I totally understand. Life gives us the hand we are dealt. It's up to us to run with it how we see fit. I would never do anything different. My daughter is my world, as well. Do you ever wonder what happened to the person you were truly in love with?"

How do I say this without telling her that it's her? "Sometimes I do but, in the end, she had to do what was best for her. If I learned nothing else in life, it's that there's no going back. There are no do-overs, only tomorrow is another day to try and do better." She curls up next to me with her wine and a blanket and mindlessly flips through the television channels.

chapter
NINETEEN

Amelia

T HIS WEEK HAS BEEN A WHIRLWIND. THE BEST PART
is—I've gotten to spend most of it with Mitch. I'm even
more excited to head out this weekend. Chloe is on her
way here to pick up Rusty until I get back. I don't know who's
more excited: Rusty or me. He's staring out my bedroom
window as I'm finishing up the last of my packing. I can tell
Chloe must be close because Rusty does the wiggle butt
whenever she is here. When she gets to the steps, he takes off
running. I finish up and head downstairs, knowing she's going
to give me the third degree.

"Hey, Chloe, thanks for taking care of him for me. I have
his bag all packed up for you."

"Don't even think of rushing me out of here. Don't lie; do

you still have a thing for him?" I roll my eyes and start tidying up the kitchen. Anything to avoid this conversation.

"What makes you think I have a thing for him. We are friends, that's all, so don't make something out of nothing."

"So, if I open that overnight bag, will I find some sexy shit?"

"If my oversized Springsteen shirt is sexy shit, then yes." She rolls her eyes and grabs Rusty's leash.

"I'm out of here. I hope you find what you're looking for!" she yells as she's running out the door. I know she's pissed at all of Peter's friends for not coming around, but that's their choice. Not everyone knows what to say. Hell, I wouldn't know what to say. I head to the front door to wait for Mitch only to see him outside with Chloe. She seems to be yelling at and poking him in the chest. Do I rescue him or let her have her say? Oh hell, he's a big boy; he can handle it. Instead I fill up two travel mugs with tea. By the time I'm done, Chloe is gone, and Mitch is knocking on the door. When I open it, I notice, in the sunlight, the deep lines etched on his forehead.

"Hey, how bad did she tear into you?"

"Nothing that I can't handle. She has your best interests at heart, but she can be a tough one."

"You'll either get used to her or run away." I shrug. "I'm ready to go. If you take my bag, I can take the tea."

He loads the car and opens the door for me. Something I'm not use to. "Let the fun begin, Amelia."

Chloe

The more I think about Mitch, the more pissed I get. I know I should mind my own business, but I can't, I never could. However, there is one person who, unfortunately, I realized too late, can't lie to save his life . . . not even to me. I bang on Doug's door for a good fifteen minutes until his wife, Nadine, finally answers the damn thing.

"What are you doing here?"

"I have to talk to Doug. Where is he?"

"I haven't seen you in well over twenty years, since that night you walked in on me and Doug, and now you want to talk to him? Fuck you." She tries to slam the door in my face, but Rusty lets out a wail that stops her in her tracks.

"I mean business, Nadine. Where is he?"

"Maybe if you meant business that night, you would be his wife and not me."

It takes all of me not to punch her in her face. In the corner of my eye, I see Doug walking up the block. Oh, I really missed out big on this one. Thank you, God, for always having my back. I turn and head down the steps, leaving her in the doorway.

When I get close enough to him, he stops and stares at me and then Rusty. He tries to step around me. "Doug Kane, stop walking, right now. I have some questions for you. I don't need your wife listening, so let's walk and talk."

"After all these years, now you want to talk? What about the day you called me a useless prick and walked away? You never even stayed to hear my side of the story. She got me piss ass drunk and convinced me I was on my way to marrying you,

Chloe. I was so drunk, that's what I thought I did. Instead, when my long bender was over, I found myself married to the hag."

"If that's the case, then why did you stay with her?"

"She was pregnant, and, unlike Peter, I wouldn't walk out on a pregnant wife."

"That's a low blow, even for you. I didn't believe you then and I don't believe you now. Besides, it all worked out for the best. Now what about Mitch? He always had a thing for Amelia. All of the sudden, he's sniffing around. Why? What's in it for him? Please don't tell me he wants to rekindle their relationship or some bullshit like that."

"You'd have to talk to him and find out why. I'm not his keeper."

"Bullshit, and I already did. He gave some lame excuse. Did you ever tell him about us?"

"No. At the time, I didn't want to look like some lame ass pussy to my friends. Besides, right after that, Peter married Amelia. Mitch was the last of us to get married. Did you tell Amelia about me?"

"I told her I knew you from the neighborhood but you're an ass, so stay away. Do you know what happened to Peter that night? If you do, just tell me already. You know everything that goes on in the neighborhood, even Peter's business, so tell me the truth."

"I can't."

"Can't or won't?!"

"Maybe a little bit of both."

"Is he alive?! Do you know where he is and you're not telling?"

"I don't know anything; I only know what you know. I just don't believe anyone would walk out on a seven-month pregnant woman. What do you think happened that night?"

I'm trying to read between the lines but with Doug, it's always been so hard when he's got his stone-cold face on. I usually can tell when he's lying but right now, I'm on the fence. I knew that day I walked in on him that he was telling the truth. He was so drunk, I'm surprised he was able to get it up. Problem is, the picture of Doug's cock in that slut was burned in my brain forever. "Doug, I thought about it for a long time; I think he's dead, but I don't know why anyone would want to kill him. It's not like he was rich, famous, or anything like that. Plus, why torch the car with no body in it?"

"I thought the same thing. When everything happened, Mitch and I searched everywhere we could think of, but we came up empty. I have no idea how someone could be gone without a trace. I even had a friend of mine on the police force, whose sister works for witness protection, check to see if that's what happened to him—nothing."

I know Doug. There's more. But, at this point, he's not about to give me anything. "I'm not going to stop digging, no matter what. Take care of yourself, Doug, and tell Mitch he better watch his back. He broke her heart once, I'll be damn if I let him do it again," I warn. He starts to say something but, at this moment, I don't believe anything. Rusty and I make our way to the car and head home.

chapter
TWENTY-ONE

Amelia

THE FLIGHT WASN'T BAD, AND OUR RENTAL CAR WAS waiting for us. I booked us at a very cute bed and breakfast. Since I'm the one who booked it, I didn't want to seem presumptuous that we are sharing a room. So now, with the help of the owner, it looks like we got the last room left. Truth is, I let him slip through my fingers once, and I want to try and make up for it. I knew the day we ran into each other at the courthouse that *it* was still there. I let Peter take control of my life back then, but not anymore. I'm the only one who is at the wheel. He's dead, and I'm driving this bus . . . hopefully, it's not off a cliff.

"Amelia, I can call around and see if there are any hotels that have something available."

"No, we are adults; don't be ridiculous. I'd rather hit the ground running. There is a lot of exploring to do, not just the houses." That seems to satisfy him. We leave the stuff in the room unpacked. He takes my hand, making my stomach do a flip. As we head out the door, the owner gives me a wink and a smile.

He has the printouts of the houses that I found and he's flipping through them. He's got on tight fitting jeans, a pull-over sweater in a royal blue that brings out the blue in his eyes.

"Do you have a special order you want to go in? Hello, Amelia, did I lose you?"

"Sorry I was just worried about Rusty." Thank goodness I'm quick on my feet.

"Is this the first time you're leaving him with Chloe?"

"No, I always worry when I have to leave him. Why don't we pick the one that's furthest away and work our way back here?"

With his hand in mine, we head out on our adventure.

After seeing six houses, we head back to the bed and break-fast to get something to eat and figure out my options. We stumble upon a quirky little eatery within walking distance to our place. I don't know what I was expecting, but we ended up with barbecue ribs, hush puppies, slaw, collards, beer, and baked apples. This was totally different from any kind of Brooklyn food.

"You know, if you move here, you're going to have to get

use to this kind of food. In New York, you have access to anything and everything twenty-four-seven. You won't have that here."

"Everything is going to be different, but that's what I wanted. I'm tired of the stress and angst of everyday life in New York. Don't you ever want to get away from it?"

"I never thought about it. I've been so used to one way of living, plus, I have a business in New York."

"I read someplace that what you've done the first thirty years of your adult life is not what you end up doing the second half of your life. What do you want to do in the second half of your life?" He gets a faraway look in his eyes, like he's pondering my question.

"Photography. I've had a love for it and would eventually like to focus on that."

"What did you think of the houses we saw today? I have a favorite, but I want to know your opinion on them."

"Amelia, you have to pick the house and then I can tear it apart." He throws his head back and laughs.

"Is that why you're here, to tear apart my dream?!"

"No, sweetheart, I'm here to make your dream happen. There is nothing worse than buying a house and ending up with buyer's remorse. Think of this like House Hunters. Let the elimination process begin!"

"Okay, the one I like the best is the blue and white cottage style."

"That one is completely renovated, and it even has a she-shed. You could use the she-shed as your workshop. The only drawback is it's only two bedrooms."

"I thought about that but it's just Rusty and me. Emma

plans on staying around the Chicago area. Besides, if she did move home, I have the second bedroom."

"Yes, you do, but you wouldn't have a guest room. What if you remarried someone with children?"

"This might sound mean or terrible, but I'm done raising my child. I wouldn't mind grandchildren but, realistically, raising babies are for the young."

"What about the four-bedroom split ranch with eight acres?"

"That's a big ass house and way too much land for me. I'm one person with a dog." He goes through every house and each one I find something wrong. That is until we get back to the first one.

"So, I guess tomorrow you are putting an offer in on the blue and white cottage."

"Yes! I really think it will be great for me. A whole new life." I try to stifle my yawn with no luck.

"Come on, Amelia, it's been a long day and tomorrow will be no different." He takes my hand again and we walk back to the B&B. I'm nervous about being alone with him in the room. Damn it, the chicken in me is coming out now. When we get in the room, all I can see is that huge king size bed. I swear it looks like it grew since we left.

"I'm going to jump in the shower." I don't give him time to answer as I grab my toiletries bag and race into the bathroom. I climb into the clawfoot tub, letting the hot water cascade down my back. I thought I was so ready for this, for him. Truth be told, I'm just as nervous around him now as I was all those years ago. I can't stop thinking about what he said about being in love versus loving someone. Maybe that was the problem all along for both of us.

The water is starting to run cold. I shut it off and pull the curtain back only to find Mitch brushing his teeth. His eyes lock on mine in the mirror. When his eyes begin to slowly travel down my body in the mirror, I realize I'm naked as a jay bird. I yelp and pull the curtain in front of me. I can hear him laughing right before his hand reaches in with a towel. "Thank you."

"No big deal. Remember, you're the one who said we were adults." He takes my hand and helps me out of the tub. When he reaches in to turn on the water, the towel that I didn't notice around his waist, falls. I try to look away . . . really, I do. Oh hell, he's got such a tight ass. I'm proud of myself for *not* looking away.

"Do you like the view?" He climbs into the tub and pulls the curtain closed.

"As a matter of fact, I do." I throw on my Springsteen shirt and with a beet red face, head into bed. The more I sit here and stew, the more I want to jump him the minute he comes out of the bathroom. Selling a house, buying a house, moving out of state, and on top of all of that, a man that I've had feelings for long before Peter and I got married is now naked in the bathroom. He's getting ready to join me *in this bed!* I really need to slow this down. I have an idea on just how to do it. I look in the dresser and find a flat sheet. I pull out two of the clothespins I have with me that have a hook to hang it. I took them with me so I could wash my bras and hang them up to dry. I hook the sheet to the headboard and footboard, so it makes a sort of pony wall. The bathroom door opens, and he steps out. He doesn't move.

"Mitch, you can come in."

"I thought I was in that movie *It Happened One Night.*"

"I love classic movies. That's where I got the idea. Our situation here reminded me of that movie. I hope you don't mind."

"Of course not, as long as you're comfortable." He climbs into his side of the bed and peeks around the curtain. "Good night, sweetheart. Sweet dreams."

I pull the covers up to my chin. I don't know why I'm embarrassed. It's like I've been transported back in time to when I first met him. I turn off the light next to the bed and try to get some sleep.

chapter
TWENTY-ONE

Mitch

I'M LYING IN BED, TRYING NOT TO LAUGH. SHE WAS SO adamant about sharing the room and being an adult, yet, she chickened out in the end. If I wanted to, I could push the case, but I don't want to scare her away. Besides, she decided she's moving out of New York. Even if she wanted me, I don't know that I'm ready to do that. When you've only lived one place your whole life, it's all you really know. Moving out of New York reminds me of the movie *Goodfellas* when Henry Hill goes into witness protection and ends up in some midwestern state eating jar tomato sauce. Not that there is anything wrong with that, if that's what you know, but when you grow up on one type of sauce and then you can't have it, it freaks you the fuck out. Peter's finally out of the picture, to Brook, Becky is dating. Amelia is trying to move on with her life. I'm the one who is stuck ... stuck in the past, remembering a love that was lost. I peek around the sheet again to find her fast asleep. I inch my way closer toward her and take her hand. I refuse to let life pass me by again. Back then, it was Peter's time. Right here, right now, it's my time. I squeeze her hand a little tighter as I drift off to sleep.

I had the best sleep of my life. When I open my eyes, I realize I'm spooned up against her. The sheet is down and in between us, her hand still in mine. I'm not sure how we got into this position, but I know I don't want to break the connection. My morning hard on feels the same way. I nuzzle into her neck. Her hair smells amazing, like citrus and flowers. I'm sniffing like some sort of lunatic when I hear her giggle. I freeze, knowing I've been busted.

"Good morning, Mitch, is there some reason you're sniffing my hair?" I'm about to pull away when she pulls me closer toward her.

"I woke up wrapped in you and your hair was everywhere. It smells like an orange orchard surrounded by wildflowers." She pushes her beautiful butt back a little, which hits me square in my morning wood. I think I might explode from something that simple.

"Well, I hope you like it."

"Very much." I need to get my mind off what I want to do to her right now. "After we put an offer on the house, what would you like to do?"

"I want to explore the town. Oh, if we can get tickets to The Biltmore, I would like to go."

"Okay, I'm going to jump in the shower and then, while you're getting ready, I'll put the offer in on the house. I'll also put your house in the MLS. I'll bet by the time we get home we'll have multiple offers." Not that it matters, I'll make sure my holding company buys the house.

Amelia

It's our last night in Asheville. To say this trip has been a whirl-wind is putting it mildly. My offer was accepted on the house in Asheville. I got a full cash offer on my house in New York. I'm going to be able to pay cash for my new house. I never lived without a mortgage payment. I have to get a car, but after that, I'm investing the rest. I want to be able to live off of my up-salvage business. I don't want to plan too much in advance. Sometimes, plans go awry. The Biltmore was everything I expected and more. I can't wait to see it at Christmas time. We've been walking on a trail in the park. When we come to a bench, he takes my hand and we sit for a while.

"Amelia, you're daydreaming again. You seem to do that a lot. Tell me what you're thinking."

I turn towards him. He reaches in and tucks my hair behind my ear. "I can't stop thinking about the future. All of the opportunities it holds. I wonder if Peter were still alive, would he want to move?"

"I don't think Peter would have ever left New York. He

always loved the ocean. If anything, he would have bought a boat."

I tilt my head and cock my eyebrows. It's something I do when confused. I never realized it until Emma imitated me. It's amazing what we learn from our children and, yet, we supposedly teach them. "He told me you guys worked one summer on a yacht, but I didn't know he had such a love for the ocean. It makes me wonder what else I don't know."

"I don't think he would hide it from you. Maybe the opportunity to share it with you never came up."

"Oh, Mitch, you always did give everyone the benefit of the doubt, even me. Maybe that's why I always felt so comfortable with you." I offer him a smile. He pulls my hand to his lips and gently kisses it. My hand trembles at the touch of his lips.

"Do I make you nervous, Amelia?"

He gently strokes the side of my face with his fingertips. When he runs his thumb over my lips, I close my eyes, take his hand and kiss it like he did mine. "I'm not nervous, just unsure of myself."

"Why? You are a beautiful lady with a lot to offer."

"Honestly, when I first met you guys, I was young and impressionable. You and I were finally getting to know each other and then Peter blew in. He was like a hurricane, totally disrupting my world. Within weeks, we were married. It wasn't what I was looking for. Hell, I was trying to get from point A to point B unscathed. Somewhere in between there, I lost you. The thought that I might have hurt you really bothered me. I was hoping after Peter disappeared that I would see you again and find the balls to apologize to you. You never came back, though, so I figured maybe it wasn't meant to be. Maybe the thought of hurting you was just in my own imagination." I fidget. He's very quiet. His blue eyes seem even bluer and more intense.

"Amelia, why don't we walk for a bit." He gets up, taking me with him.

"We don't have to talk about it, if you don't want to."

"I want to. I just need to walk for a bit. I was hurt—very hurt. I thought you and I had something. You know, working towards more. What that was, I had no idea. I wanted to find out, though. Then Peter bulldozed his way through our relationship. When he announced out of the blue that you were engaged, I stepped away."

"Why? Why didn't you tell me how you really felt?"

"Would it have made a difference? Besides, that's what best friends do. They give their friend every chance at happiness."

"Do you think he would have done the same thing for you?"

"Back then, yes. But now I'm not so sure."

"I guess we will never know. It's in the past, maybe we should leave it there. You know, maybe start fresh like we just met. I would like that, if you would."

He smiles and I could swear there is a glint in his eyes. "Hi, Amelia, I'm Mitch, very nice to meet you." He extends his hand, allowing me to slip mine into it. "Very nice to meet you, Mitch."

chapter
TWENTY-TWO

Mitch

WHEN WE FINALLY GOT BACK TO BROOKLYN. I offered to take her to pick up Rusty, but Chloe was already at her house with him. She was excited to tell Chloe everything. I was going to stay but I wanted to call Brook before it got any later. I want to start a new relationship with Amelia, but not only is she moving to another state, I have a huge secret that can change everything. This is why I hate secrets. I'm about to pull into my garage when Doug comes down the steps to talk to me before I pull into the garage.

"Careful on those steps, Doug, you're not getting any younger."

"Fuck you, asshole. What happened in Asheville?"

I'm not about to tell him what happened between Amelia and me. "She bought a house. She's moving in thirty days. I put her house up for sale and the holding company made her a cash offer, just like we talked about. She took it, so in thirty days, we can start tearing apart the house."

"Why do I feel there is something more that you're not telling me?"

"Maybe because you watch too many soap operas. Stop reading into everything."

"Come on, Mitch, this isn't my first rodeo—spill!"

"I feel guilty not telling her about the heist. After spending so much time with her, I realized she really didn't know him at all. Hell, she didn't even know about his love of the ocean."

"Do you ever wonder why the hell he even married her?"

"The more I talk to her, the more I wonder." I check my watch and if I don't call Brook now, it will be too late. "I've got to run and call Brook. I'll talk to you in the morning." I rush him off. He grumbles under his breath as he heads back up the steps. If he doesn't do something about his health, I'll be the only one left of the musketeers to spend the loot. I sit down with a nice cognac and call my daughter.

"Hey, Daddy, how was the weekend with Amelia?"

Subtly is not her strong suit. "It was a nice, relaxing weekend. Two old friends getting reacquainted. In the process, I sold her house here and helped her purchase a new one in Asheville."

"Did you get to The Biltmore? I heard it's fantastic. Benjamin and I want to take a trip there."

"The Biltmore was everything it was pumped up to be and more. So, how is Benjamin?"

"He's fine, Dad. When will you be coming up to meet him?"

"I was waiting for you to tell me when. You could come home and bring him with you."

"That might be a better idea. Then I can show him around before we go to Jacksonville to meet his parents."

My jaw is tight, and I feel my left eye twitch. That's usually not a good sign. "You're already going to meet his parents. I thought you were going to take it slow, test the waters." I throw her words back at her.

"We have spring break coming up, and Florida was on our list. I'll talk Benjamin in to stopping in Brooklyn first. So, back to Amelia, do you think you will see her again . . . other than work?"

"She's moving out of state in thirty days. Not sure how starting a relationship at this point would be the smart thing to do."

"Have you ever thought of retiring and moving out of Brooklyn?"

"I can't just up and move on a whim, Brook. I'm too old; that ship sailed a long time ago. Can we please change the subject? When will you be here?"

"Ugh, you are so pigheaded. We will be there Saturday, satisfied?"

"Thank you. Well, I just got home, so I've got a lot to catch up on. I'll see you Saturday. Love you."

"Love you too, Daddy."

Truth is, I really have nothing to do, but I didn't want to keep getting the third degree about Amelia. Brook wants answers, answers that I don't have. I feel like I have the devil on one shoulder and the angel on the other. All I know is, no matter what happens, I'm screwed. It's just how long I put off the inevitable.

Brook

"Brook, what's the matter? You're walking around here banging stuff and talking under your breath."

"I just got off the phone with my dad, need I say anything more?"

"Did you tell him we are coming down on Saturday?"

"Benjamin, think of who you're talking to; of course, I told him."

"So, what's the problem?"

"Amelia, that's the problem. I know my dad is stalling, I just can't figure out why. He's single, she's single. It's so obvious they like each other. If they would just get out of their own way, maybe they would have a shot at something good."

"You can't make them do something if they aren't ready. You keep wanting to manipulate the situation the way you think it should be, but that's not always what the universe has planned."

"Yeah, yeah, I get it. It doesn't mean I have to like it. I would call Emma, but she is a lot like her mom. She's a very laid back, *what will be, will be* sort. Anyway, did you call your parents to tell them we are coming down?"

"Yes, my sister is over the moon and can't wait to meet you."

I laugh a high-pitched, nervous laugh, nothing like my usual laugh. The thought of meeting his whole family makes my heart race. It's just another thing on my plate. "What if they don't like me? I'm from a middle-class family in Brooklyn. What if they think I'm not good enough?"

"You are being ridiculous. They will love you. I love you. They are happy I'm finally bringing someone home."

"So, as long as I'm breathing, I pass the test?"

He lifts me up and carries me to the living room. We have a balcony that looks out over the city. "Benjamin, I just got done at the gym; I need a shower.

"I can feel your breath on my neck, so you pass the test," he says. I want to be mad, but I can't help but laugh. He puts me down and spins me around so I'm looking out over the city. He slips his fingers under my workout bra and he pulls it off.

"Put your hands on the glass and don't move." He's behind me slowly peeling off my sweats.

"Benjamin, don't you think people can see us?" I ask as his hands travel up my torso.

"Does it make you excited that people you don't know are watching me tweak your nipples." He tugs at them and my knees begin to buckle. He pushes me up against the cold glass. When my nipples press against the glass, I feel a chill run over my entire body. He spreads my legs and his fingers caress the inside of my thighs. He drops to his knees and nips at my ass. First one side and then the other.

"Ohhhh yes!"

"How many men do you think are watching as my hand slowly works its way into your pussy? How many women do you think wish they were you right now?"

He gets up off his knees as my hands begin to slide down the glass. That gets me five stinging slaps on my ass. This is the side to Benjamin I love the most: the dominant side that makes me forget about everything else. He forces me to give up all control.

"Do it again and I'll use the belt."

My hands quickly slide back up the glass. I hate the belt, but I love his hands. Just the right sting, the border between pain and pleasure. I see his reflection in the glass. I can feel my skin begin to prickle as he trails his fingers up and down my spine. He slowly smiles. He always says he loves my ass and as he traces the handprints that I know he left there, my whole body flushes. Watching his reflection is such a turn on. It's like watching a movie that I'm staring in.

"Push your ass back for me," he commands. I turn my head to look at him and realize that was a no-no as his hand comes down hard. First one cheek and then the other.

"If I wanted you to look, I would tell you. I can see you're watching our reflection in the door. How many people do you think, Brook? Put your hands on your breasts and put them on display for everyone to see."

I push back slowly taking my hands off the glass and wrap them around my breasts.

"Now, play with your nipples—pull them—hard."

I lean my forehead against the cold glass as I do everything he demands. I have to admit, knowing others can see me is a total turn on. I look up and he has his cock out, pumping it. He steps closer between my legs and pushes them wider, bending me just enough so he can slowly glide his cock into my pussy. He is very large and I'm petite, so I feel every inch of him. "Ughhhhh, please give me a minute," I beg. He does.

"Let me know when you're ready." His hands slowly working their way up and down my sides, trying to get me to relax.

"Okay."

He pulls back very slowly and then pushes forward, repeating until we've got a rhythm going. But then he pulls back and slams into me. "Put your hands on the glass, Brook, now!"

I do as he commands. We are back to the slow and steady pace. I'm thinking I've got this now. I was wrong. He pulls out and slams into me while striking my ass. "Fuck me hard, please," I beg. By the fifth blow, I can't hold back anymore. I don't have time to warn him; I'm coming. When I open my eyes and look in the glass, I see his head tilted back and he lets out a wail. I think it's safe to say he found his release, too. When I finally catch my breath, I turn to face him.

"Do you really think people can see us?"

He cocks his head and smirks. "Do you really think they can't?"

I might have to move!

chapter
TWENTY-THREE

Mitch

BROOK IS COMING THIS WEEKEND. NORMALLY, I WOULD be thrilled. However, she's bringing Benjamin. What exactly does that mean? She's never brought a guy home before. I don't know how I'm supposed to act. She didn't say how long she was staying. Maybe she wants to see how it goes. That's what I would do. I decide to call Amelia for advice. Okay, maybe I'm just reaching for any excuse to talk to her. I think this is a legitimate excuse.

"Hey, Amelia, I need to bounce something off of you. Do you have time?"

"Sure. I'm home, if you want to come over."

I'm not going to let that opportunity pass me by. "I'll head right over. Do you need me to bring anything?"

"I just opened a bottle of red, unless you want something else."

"Nope, red is great. I'll be right over." I quickly check myself before heading out.

Luckily, I'm only a few minutes away.

"Hey, that was quick. Come on in." She opens the door fully, allowing me to enter. We head into her living room where a bottle and two empty glasses wait. She pours me a glass of wine once we sit, and we curl up on the couch. Rusty jumps up, giving me the stare down. "So, what's up? Is everything with the house okay?"

"Oh yeah, everything is fine. This is personal parenting stuff. I need advice. Brook is bringing a guy home this weekend. She's never brought anyone home before. What does this mean and how the hell am I supposed to act?" I spill it out. She's biting her bottom lip and it seems like she's trying not to laugh. "I'm serious, Amelia, I've never had this problem before."

"Well, I'm sure Brook has dated before, how did you handle that?"

"She dated but she never brought anyone home for me to meet. The guy moved in with her, which goes against my beliefs, but I'm trying really hard not to be judgmental. I know I'm old school and my beliefs are not hers. She made that clear when she said she doesn't want to end up in a marriage like mine."

"Ouch, how did you handle that?"

"I threw up."

"Really?"

"Well, almost. I told you—I'm old school."

"Is that part of the reason you never came around after Peter disappeared?"

I've got a death grip on my glass. I think this might be a

good time to clear the air. "That is part of the reason I never came around. I loved my wife; she gave me Brook. You and I, we had unfinished business. I knew if I came around, things would happen, and I was a married man. I didn't trust myself. I respected my wife and my morals." I watch her face as she listens to my confession. She gives nothing away.

"Back then, I had feelings for you. Feelings that we never got to explore. Our timing was off. Honestly, we are both free now and I wouldn't mind exploring them. You know, see where it leads. What's the other part?"

"The other part is, you're moving away in less than thirty days! It seems like our timing is always going to be off."

"It's only off if we let it be. People have long distance relationships that work. North Carolina is not that far away. But let's table that for now and work on your problem. Why are you so afraid? You raised Brook to be a street-smart independent lady. She wouldn't bring someone home if she didn't feel he could pass muster with you."

"See, you make it sound so simple. What the hell am I supposed to talk to him about? *'Hey how is sleeping with my daughter going?'* Do you see what I mean? I can't get past that."

"Mitch, I'm going to give you the best piece of advice ever. Get your head out of your ass. Be happy that your daughter respects you enough to even bring him home! Talk to the guy about school and what he plans on doing after graduation. Stuff like that, and you'll be fine."

"Will you come over when they are here? You know, for moral support."

"Chicken shit. Yes, I will be there as long as Brook is okay with it. When are they coming down?"

"This Saturday."

"Lucky for you I don't have a life." She laughs and I can't help but laugh along with her.

"Do you really think a long-distance relationship could work?" *Of course, it could work, you idiot, as long as you tell her the truth. Unfortunately, you keep digging that hole deeper and deeper.*

"I think any relationship can work if two people put one-hundred percent into it. It begins with honesty and trust. At this stage in my life, I won't settle for anything less."

I put my glass down and pull her close to me. I brush my lips across hers, she slightly parts them and that's my cue. Our tongues do a dance and I feel lightheaded. I pull back slightly and brush my hand across her cheek. "You are so beautiful."

"You are very kind, Mitch."

She pours more wine in her glass, but I put my hand over my glass. "I have to drive home."

"Or you could stay. We've got the whole sheet between us thing down!" She winks. I remove my hand and let her fill it up.

"Have you been researching cars?"

"They've changed a lot in twenty years. I'm looking for an SUV, and I want to buy resale. I want something that will hold its value and be low maintenance. Do you have any suggestions?"

"You've been in my Lexus, did you like it?"

"I did, but I think I want to go test drive some different vehicles this week."

"Do you want me to go with you? I mean, after all, you're helping me out this weekend."

"Sure, that would be great. Would you like to watch a movie?"

"Sure, I've been wanting to see The Irishman. It's on demand. Have you seen it?"

"No, you want to see it because you're Irish." She's laughing and when she does, her face lights up. All these years that Peter's been gone, he missed so much. He missed this, a beautiful woman and a daughter who is very special.

"Guilty as charged. It's a long movie, but I heard good things about it."

"Okay, you get it ready and I'll make some popcorn." She heads into the kitchen and I set up the movie. I'm comfortable, more comfortable than I've been in years. It's like I was transferred back in time to when all I cared about was her. I ask myself every day why I didn't fight for her. Loyalty to my best friend. He told me he loved her, and he wanted her forever. I should have told him that I loved her, too. Instead, he showed me the ring and I backed off. It's been said nice guys finish last. Maybe, but I'm alive and with Amelia. Peter is, for all intents and purposes, dead.

"Okay, since it's a really long movie, I made caramel popcorn."

The movie is good, but she is amazing.

chapter
TWENTY-FOUR

Amelia

THE MOVIE IS OVER, THE POPCORN IS GONE, THE SECOND bottle of wine is empty, and Mitch is fast asleep. I don't have the heart to wake him. Instead, I cover him with a throw and Rusty curls up by his feet . . . *traitor*.

I head upstairs, running everything that happened to-night in my head. I don't understand why he is holding back. Even though he seems open to a long-distance relationship, something is off, and I can't put my finger on it. I don't know why he's so worried about meeting Brook's boyfriend. I mean, Emma has brought some guys home, but they didn't last, and I knew they wouldn't. Maybe he's afraid Brook will shut him out of her life. She doesn't seem the type, though. He's got to realize that his relationship with her will change many times over the course of his life. I'll make sure I pay attention to their interaction on Saturday. I'm glad he's going to go with me for the car. I kept my license for twenty years, but I haven't driven, so this could be very interesting. I left that part out not wanting to scare him away. I don't think I would drive in New York, but I think I'll be okay in Asheville, I hope.

It took a long time for me to fall asleep last night. However, the smell of bacon is overwhelming. I have a nice long stretch and then open my eyes. Mitch is sitting on the edge of the bed with a tray.

"Oh, wow, what a spectacular way to wake up. Bacon, coffee, biscuits, eggs, and a chocolate chip cookie."

"I'm sorry about last night. I was so comfortable, I fell into such a deep sleep. That is until Rusty began licking my face."

"That usually means he's already went outside and did his business and now he wants to eat."

"I figured that and made him eggs. I hope that's okay."

I can't help but laugh. "He played you like a fiddle. Are you joining me?"

"I can't. I've got a closing later and stuff to do to get ready for it. Figure out when you want to go for the car."

"Okay. I'll probably wait until I'm ready to leave. I don't want it sitting here. What time will Brook get in?"

"I'm not sure but I'll let you know as soon as I find out. Thanks for being there for me. I know I'm being ridiculous, but it's who I am."

He gets up, kisses me on the cheek, and heads out. At

least I got a breakfast in bed. Rusty comes in, jumps on the bed and begins to beg. "Don't even try to give me that sad look. I know you already had breakfast." He gives up, curls up and watches to see if I drop anything. Fat chance, Rusty.

Mitch

I head to Doug's house, knowing he's probably watching by his window for me to come home. We look out for each other, not just because we are friends, more because we are nosey. The minute I pull up, he comes out the door still in his robe. He walks outside to get his paper and gives me the finger when he goes back inside. It's times like this he reminds me of Vincent Gigante, the mafia leader who feigned insanity and walked around Greenwich Village in his bathrobe for years. I swear Doug is turning into him. I climb his steps to find he left the door open for me.

"Where were you last night? You want coffee?"

I don't answer since I already know he's going to give me a cup. "I need to talk to you about something important."

"First, tell me where you were last night. I was waiting up for you."

"You're not my father and what the hell are you doing—channeling your inner Vincent Gigante? Stop walking around outside in your bathrobe," I remark. He waves his hand, dismissing me and pushes the cup toward me.

"So, are you going to tell me where you were? Is that better?"

I can't help but laugh at him. "I went to Amelia's house and fell asleep watching a movie."

"What the fuck is wrong with you? You're playing with fire. You need to let her go for good."

"See, that's what I want to talk to you about. I've got a thing for her."

"Ha, why don't you tell me something I don't know?"

"I don't want to let her go. I want to tell her everything. She wants to have a relationship and so do I. Unfortunately, you know me, I can't have a relationship based on lies. Every move I make compounds one lie on top of another. See, that's the thing about lying, once you start, you keep making up more to hide the original one. After a while, you can't even remember where it started. I feel like I'm in a house of cards that's about to collapse around me."

"So, you want to tell her about the heist. Tell her that our holding company purchased her house, so we can tear it apart looking for the jewels. Exactly how do you think that's going to go over?"

"I don't know, but I can't go on like this."

"Once you tell her, she'll tell Chloe. From there, all bets are off."

"We can't go to jail since there is nothing to show that we did the heist."

"She'll blame us for Peter. Whether he left on his own accord or if he was murdered, either way, she'll be playing the blame game."

"What about Chloe? Wasn't she hanging around with you at that time? What does she know?"

"She knows nothing. I met her after the heist. By the time

you and Peter brought Amelia around, Chloe already walked out on me."

The mention of her name makes him sit up ram rod straight. I don't think he'll ever tell me what happened between them. Truthfully, I don't want to know. I have enough of my own secrets to keep, I don't need any more.

"Brook is coming home this weekend. She's bringing her boyfriend Benjamin home for me to meet. I asked Amelia if she would be there with me."

"Is that why you want to spill your guts, because she wants to be there for you at a moment's notice, or is it all the lies that are making you feel guilty?"

"When did I become such a Dudley Do Right?"

"You always were. Peter and I are the ones that took you to the dark side." He laughs. I roll my eyes and get up to for more coffee.

"You're not helping me at all."

"At the end of the day, I can't tell you what to do. Remember, I'm not your father. You'll do what's best for you. If you tell her everything, you stand a good chance of losing her. If you don't tell her everything, it will eat you up inside and you'll be miserable. In the end, it will fracture your relationship, and you'll lose her."

"So, I'm fucked either way."

"That about sums it up. Now, why don't you tell me what's going on with Brook. This is the first time she's bringing someone home to meet you. I want to be there, too. I mean, after all, I am her Godfather."

"The guy moved in with her," I announce. Doug's face turns red as a beet. Maybe I should have eased into that more.

"Oh, fuck no. Did you talk to her about this?"

"After I fought the urge to throw up, I had to listen to her version of what she thought my marriage was all about. I don't have to tell you, since you've lived it too in your own marriage. All in all, she made me realize I'm a lousy liar. After that, there was really nothing left to be said."

"Ouch, that had to hurt, man. I'm sorry."

"It's my own fault. I married a woman I wasn't in love with. I love her for giving me Brook, but that's it."

"Yeah, like me and the hag. So, how do you think Amelia is going to help you out with the meet and greet?"

"You have such a way with words. I just don't want to be alone when I meet him. I need someone to keep me in check."

"What am I, chopped liver? I plan on being there!"

"You're already pissy about the guy moving in with her. You'll only add fuel to the fire."

"I promise you I'll behave. Well, only if he's good enough for my Goddaughter."

"I've got to go. We have the closing on the house on East 48th street today. Once I have the keys, I'll drop them off and you can get started with flipping it." We actually have a legitimate business where we buy and flip houses. I put my cup in the sink and head out, leaving him to his paper.

chapter
TWENTY-FIVE

TODAY'S THE DAY I MEET BENJAMIN. I DON'T KNOW WHY I'm so nervous. I made up my mind that as long as he is a good person and good to my daughter, I'll accept their arrangement. Who am I to judge? I think I'll go pick up Amelia instead of her taking an Uber.

Me: Hey, sweetheart, I'm going to come and get you, so you don't have to Uber.

Amelia: Please don't be mad but I've got the flu. I've been kissing the porcelain god since last night. I was hoping it was a twenty-four-hour bug, but I still have a fever today.

Me: I could never be mad at you. Do you want me to bring you some soup or something?

Amelia: No! I don't want you getting sick. Don't worry about today. You'll do great ... promise.

Me: Okay, rest up and I'll check in later.

Amelia: Thanks.

Well hell, I'm on my own. Doug doesn't count because you never know which way he's going to go. Speak of the devil, he's coming up the walk now.

"Hey, Amelia has the flu, so it's just us."

"I called Vanni to see if she could shed some light on this guy. She warned me it's Benjamin not Ben. She said she talks about him all the time. They are supposed to come to Dallas for a visit soon."

"Brook warned me about the Ben thing, too. We got this, right, Doug?"

"Are you asking me or reassuring yourself?"

I hear a car door and I don't know if I'm excited for my daughter or nervous for myself. She's already up the steps and then he comes into view. I'm looking at him and then to Doug. Brook is making the introductions, but I can't focus on her. All I see is his face, a face I've seen before. I hear a crash; Doug dropped his glass. His face is pale as he grabs the back of the dining room chair.

"Uncle Doug, are you okay? Daddy, should we call an ambulance?"

I put a chair behind him, and he sits down. He won't look at anyone but Benjamin. "Brook, get him a glass of water, please."

When she comes back, I take the glass and step in front of Doug. I need to stop him from staring. He takes the glass and closes his eyes. The color is finally coming back to his face. "Brook, why don't you take Benjamin and show him around." Luckily, she doesn't question me. When they are out of ear shot, I bend down in front of Doug. Before I can say anything, he grabs my arm and has a death grip on it.

"Mitch, tell me you see what I see, please."

"Yeah, but how is that even possible?"

"It can't be; Peter is dead. I feel like I was transported back in time twenty years."

"Where's the picture, Doug? Don't say you don't know. I know for a fact you've never let that photo out of your sight." He pulls out his wallet and pulls out the wrinkled picture. It was the night after the heist. I got a new camera for the trip and wanted to take a group photo. I set the timer. We all stood there waiting and right before the camera flashed, Peter threw two fists filled with diamonds up the air. The photo that captured the whole thing.

"Look at it closely, Mitch. It's him, it's Peter."

"No, Doug, he's got to be Peter's son, and he's fucking my daughter!"

"We better go inside before Brook comes to get us. Are you okay?"

"Yeah, I need to talk to this kid. Don't worry, I won't give anything away."

We find them downstairs in what's now the Man Cave.

"Uncle Doug, are you okay?"

"Yeah, I didn't eat much today, and I got a little light-headed. So, Benjamin, tell me, where did you grow up?"

"Jacksonville, Florida. My dad has a business there. He runs it with my mom. It's a food truck but on the water. My dad wanted to live in a houseboat but my mom drew the line in the sand on that one, so that's how the Diamond Reef food boat became a reality and my dad gets to spend most of his days being out on the water."

"So, a food boat. Very interesting. Do you have any

siblings? My daughter and Brook are only children. They grew up together, so they are like sisters. Vanni is older than Brook. How old are you?"

"I have a younger sister. She skipped a grade and is a senior in high school. I'm six months older than Brook."

I need to steer the conversation away from Doug's interrogation. "Wow, Benjamin, the New England winters must have been a real shock for you."

"The first year was brutal. I'm used to it now, but who knows where we will end up when we graduate."

"Do you have any off-limit places?" Good to know, since my daughter will be following him for sure.

"No, we are open right now. It depends who comes up with the best offer."

"When are you heading down to your parents' house?"

He looks at Brook, takes her hand. "We were able to get a cheap flight, but we have to leave tonight. I promise next time we will stay longer."

I'm watching my daughter as he's speaking to me; he's got her wrapped around his finger. This is so not like Brook. She's a strong person, yet, with this guy, she seems very different. I need to see more of an interaction between the two of them, not just a few hours.

"Well, you've got to do what works best for both of you. Why don't we go upstairs and eat an early dinner?"

We head upstairs, and I thank God I thought to buy cold cuts and rolls. It was supposed to be lunch for tomorrow, but since they are leaving, I can at least feed them. Brook helps me set everything up, including the antipasto.

"Daddy, I'm sorry about the quick trip but we couldn't

pass up the deal on the tickets. I promise you we will come back soon, or you can come up to us."

I pull her into a hug not wanting to let her go. "It's okay, at least I got to meet him and see you. Does he make you happy?"

"So far, yes, but I don't want to jinx it."

"I'll get them in here while you finish setting the table."

Surprisingly, everything is going well. Benjamin is very polite, and Doug has finally stopped with the fifty questions. Brook makes the coffee and I put out the cannoli.

"Before you leave, I'd like to get a group photo. I got a new phone and it has a feature where I can set the timer to take a photo. I'll get to test it out."

"Dad, I'm surprised you got a new phone. You hate all kinds of technology."

"I'm trying to get into this century, kicking and screaming but I'm trying."

"How's Amelia?"

"She was going to come over today, but she has the flu. I'll go check on her later. Have you spoken to Emma?"

"Yeah, she's excited about the new house. She sent me the link. It looks wonderful. Before you know it, she will be moving."

"It's coming up pretty quick. I'm taking her to buy a car. She hasn't owned a car in years and I'm not even sure when the last time she drove herself anywhere, so this should be interesting." Brook nearly chokes on her coffee.

"Daddy, remember when you tried to teach me to drive? You finally gave up and Uncle Doug had to teach me. Make sure you have patience with her."

Benjamin is looking at his watch, giving her the cue that

they have to leave. I want to make it comfortable for her even though he doesn't seem to care.

"Let's get that picture; I'm sure you need to head to the airport."

I set up the camera and take my picture. In my mind, I see Peter throwing the diamonds up in the air. We hug and kiss as they say their goodbyes. Doug and I stand on the porch, watching them drive away. When they are gone, we go inside, and Doug pulls out the photo and puts in next to the one on my phone. The two of us stare at it like it will bite us.

"Doug, you know they say everyone has a twin somewhere. What are the odds that he's Peter's twin?"

"About the same as you winning the Powerball. He's Peter's son. That is something I would bet money on."

"Thank God Amelia wasn't here tonight. This could have played out really bad." I get a knot in my gut just thinking about it.

"Mitch, maybe it's time we both sit her down and tell her the truth. I don't feel like we have a choice."

I'm staring at the photos, my mind like an old-time movie reel, playing that night over and over again.

"After today, I have to agree with you. Then, I think the three of us need to head to Jacksonville to confront the bastard." If only it was that easy. So many people are going to get hurt, including my daughter.

chapter
TWENTY-SIX

Amelia

I REALLY WANTED TO GO TO MITCH'S HOUSE YESTERDAY AND meet Brook's boyfriend. This stupid flu is kicking my ass. All I can keep down right now is tea and toast. I thought for sure I would hear from him last night but maybe he's giving me time to rest, or maybe he thinks the guy is wonderful. Nope. Knowing Mitch, I'm sure he's going to dissect the entire conversation. I'll wait a little bit longer before I text him. Maybe a long hot shower is the best thing right now. My phone beeps with a new message. I was hoping it would be Mitch but it's Chloe.

Chloe: I'm not coming by. I don't want the cooties.

Me: You're always so cheerful. I'm feeling a little better this morning, but I don't want you to catch this. Otherwise, you will never let me hear the end of it.

Chloe: Well as long as I know you're alive. Do you need me to drop off some soup or something?

Me: I'm alive. My fever broke sometime last night. Chicken matzo ball soup from the diner would be nice.

Chloe: I'll ring the bell and leave it by the door. Feel better.

Me: Thanks.

I let the hot water cascade down my back for what seems like forever. I can't wait to be doing this in my new home. Since it was a cash deal, Mitch was able to do a quick close. I did have to rent back for a couple of weeks so that I would have enough time to finish packing. I just hope this stupid flu doesn't delay any of my plans. Even though my fever is gone, I still feel like I was hit by a truck. Maybe Mitch will come by today or at least call. I want to explore what I missed with him all those years ago, but first I have to get through his wall that is keeping me at bay. The water begins to run cold, which is my sign that it's time to get out. The doorbell is ringing, it's probably Chloe dropping off my soup. The thought makes my stomach rumble. The best feeling in the world is a hot shower and then clean flannel pajamas. I head downstairs with Rusty on my heels, and when I open the door, I'm startled. Mitch and Doug are standing there, Mitch holding the soup that Chloe must have dropped off while I was in the shower. Doug, whom I haven't seen since Peter left, looks a lot older. Time has not been very kind to him.

"I'm sorry, I wasn't expecting anyone. Doug, it's been a long time." I open the door wider for them. "Please come in." I take hold of Rusty's collar, but he doesn't seem bothered by Doug, and Mitch has already won him over. I take the soup from Mitch, realizing that it will have to wait I put it in the fridge and grab some water bottles before I head into the living room. I find the two of them standing there looking very uneasy.

"Doug, I'm surprised to see you here. What's going on?" Mitch takes my hand, and leads me towards the couch. I sit down but they don't. I'm starting to get nervous.

"We have a story to tell you but please let us finish before you question us." Mitch's voice cracks.

"The year before I graduated college, I got my real estate license. We worked as a team. I would get the listings while Doug and Peter helped out when the properties needed repairs. We decided to make our last spring break our most memorable one. It was Peter and my senior year that convinced me to do so. We pooled all our money together and went on a trip of a lifetime to Cannes, France. We even got Doug to go with us. It was a few days before we were due to go home, we got very drunk and Peter came up with a plan to rob a jewelry store in a hotel. Doug and I tweaked the plan a little before we passed out." He pauses to drink some of his water, but his eyes never leave mine. Doug is rocking from one foot to the other. What he's telling me sounds like a tall tale. Kind of like the fisherman's tale of the big one that got away.

"The next day, when we sobered up, we realized we created a really good plan. I'll spare you all the details, but that night, we did it. We got the jewels home and went on with our lives. However, before that, we made a pact that we would each hold the jewels for a certain amount of time. We thought that was fair and we trusted each other, or so I thought. When Peter's turn was coming to an end, you were seven months pregnant. The night he disappeared, he was supposed to bring the jewels to me, before he went to get your stuff at the store, but he never showed up."

I jump up astonished, trying to absorb what I'm hearing. "Wait, you're telling me my husband was a jewel thief and that he skipped out on his family over money?!"

"Please, Amelia, there is a lot more. Let me finish." With my face inches from his, I'm trying to find the truth in his eyes.

"More, more, how much more could there be?! My husband was a jewel thief that vanished in the middle of the night. He put the value of stuff above the value of his daughter and his wife! Was he killed because of this? Do you know what really happened to him? Is this why you've been holding back?"

"This is very hard for me to tell you. I promise I'll answer all of your questions, but please let me finish."

I sit back down trying hard to focus on whatever else he has to tell me. My head is pounding like a freight train is running through it.

"After the torched car was found, we really thought he was murdered. We didn't think anyone would walk out on their pregnant wife. We looked everywhere we could think of to find the jewels, but we always came up empty. Fast forward to twenty years later and you had him declared legally dead. That was a break for us. I purposely ran into you on the steps of the courthouse. I needed to get into your good graces. We needed to get into this house to look around. It's the only place we weren't able to search. We thought the best thing for you to do is sell this place and the best thing for us to do is buy it, so we did."

My chin just hit the ground. I've been played like a fiddle.

THERESA SEDERHOLT

"So, let me get this straight; you bought this home just to look around? Why didn't you come to me after Peter left? There was a time I was so poor, I lived on lemon water so Emma would have food. I would have thought you were nuts, but I was so desperate, I would have looked with you. Mitch, was any of it with you real?" My heart is sinking in my chest. My feelings for him are real. What a fool I am. I get up and walk closer towards him. I don't want to miss a word he has to say.

"Yes, my feelings for you are totally real, Amelia. They always were, which is why I keep getting myself into trouble. How were we to know that you would have gone along with us?"

"Don't you mean how would you know if I would have shared the loot with you?" My instinct to protect myself takes over. I reach back and quickly smack him across the face. His face turns beet red, but Doug's facial expressions never change. He takes a step closer.

"We didn't know if we could trust you. Besides, donuts to dollars there is nothing here."

"Why are you telling me all of this now? I mean, you got away with everything from the robbery to buying my house, so why?! Are the finishing touches to this whole plot to make sure I know what a fucking fool I was?"

"This is the bad part." Mitch barely gets the words out before I'm right up in his face, again.

"You mean there's more?"

"You know yesterday Brook was bringing her boyfriend home for me to meet. I thought they were going to stay the whole weekend. Turns out they left late last night for Florida to be with Benjamin's family."

"What does that have to do with anything?"

He nudges Doug. "Show her the photos."

Doug places two photos on the coffee table. One is an old photograph and one is new photo that looks to have been recently printed. I'm staring at them and I feel my head begin to pound even harder, as if that's even possible. I pick up the old one and hold it closer. It's old and tattered but it's no mistake, the three of them are very young and there's Peter in the middle tossing into the air what looks like diamonds. When I pick up the new picture and bring it close, there is no mistaking Brook's boyfriend looks exactly like Peter did at that age. I feel the bile start to rise in my throat. I grab the photos and race to the bathroom. When I finally stop throwing up, I grab the pictures, but I can't see anything though my tears. All I have now is my uncontrollable sobbing. Staring at the photos is like a dagger in my heart. There's a light tap on the door.

"Amelia, it's Mitch. I'm by myself. Can I come in?"

I don't answer, instead, I brush my teeth and rinse my face with cold water before opening the door. "I've got questions for both of you. Living room, now!"

I'm mumbling to myself under my breath as we head into the living room. Doug is sitting in the recliner. He filled three glasses with brandy and put the bottle on the coffee table. I take one of the glasses and down it in one shot. Not the way it's supposed to be drunk. I toss the photos on the table next to the bottle. Mitch eyes the glasses of brandy, swipes one and takes a seat on the couch. His gaze is now fixated on the photos.

"I just want to get this straight before I throw you both out on your asses. You're telling me you three idiots pulled off a major robbery. My husband disappeared into the night with the jewels, and he has another family someplace. Oh, and by some divine intervention, his offspring is dating Brook. Oh, and lest I forget, you thought the jewels were hidden somewhere in this house. You bought it under false pretenses and when I leave, you're going to look for them."

"Well, after yesterday, we don't think the jewels are here. Obviously, he skipped and took them with him."

Doug gets up and takes both photos, puts them in his pocket, and turns to leave. I grab his arm and with all the force I have, spin him around. "Where the hell do you think you're going?"

"I'm going to Florida. I'm going to confront Peter, kick his ass, and get my share of the jewels." Mitch gets up, puts his empty glass down, and heads towards the door with him.

"Stop, both of you! No one is going anywhere without me. Do you understand?" They both stop and turn towards me. They aren't saying anything. Mitch is rubbing his jaw and Doug keeps looking from Mitch to me. Mitch takes a step toward me. "Well, Amelia, I guess you better get dressed."

"I'll be ready in five minutes. Oh, and we have to drop Rusty off at Chloe's house." I race upstairs with the realization that after twenty years I'm finally going to get some long-awaited answers.

Doug is driving to JFK while Mitch makes reservations for us. I'm running everything they told me over again in my head. It's a wild tale, but something is missing.

"Did anyone find out how old Benjamin is?" I notice Doug's grip on the wheel gets so tight that his knuckles are turning white.

" He told us he's six months older than Brook. Vanni was born first then Emma and lastly Brook."

He rattles off the ages of the kids, and that's when it hits me like a brick between the eyes. Not only did my husband steal the jewels from his friends, leave me all alone seven months pregnant, but he left me for another woman. A woman that had to be pregnant the same time as me. The thought makes me want to hurl or punch both these idiots in the face. I look at Doug and then to Mitch. I can see the moment the realization that Peter is a lying two-faced cheating bastard hits Mitch. His mouth drops open and his face pales. Doug, on the other hand, looks straight ahead.

"Yes, Mitch, Peter got someone else pregnant while he was married to me. It's apparent that he left me pregnant and alone for her and the jewels."

Doug looks at me in the rear-view mirror. His eyes are glaring back at me. He's not in shock like Mitch. "Amelia, I hope you get all your answers, but I wouldn't expect much from him. That ship sailed a long time ago."

chapter
TWENTY-SEVEN

Peter

SO, MY SON HAS FINALLY DECIDED TO BRING SOMEONE home. He hasn't said much to me about her. He talks more to his sister Jenny than he does to me or my wife Kelly. Everyone he's dated was always older than him but this one is six months younger. When I asked him if she's the one, he said he thought so, but she wants to wait. Imagine that; usually it's the other way around. I'm curious to see who she is or more like what she's got that has my son tossing around the L word.

The Diamond Reef was really busy this morning, but a storm is moving in and business died off very quickly. I decide to toss out my line and maybe catch something for dinner tonight while Kelly cleans up here. She steps in front of me, blocking out the sun. "Do you need me for something?" She bends down placing her hands on each side of the chair, her 36DDD's inches from my face. I paid for them and she knows how much I want access to them at all times. Hell, she gets whatever she wants, whenever she wants. As long as I can do what I want with them. I actually named them Thelma and Louise. I have to have some way to amuse myself. When she found out about the heist, she held it over my head. First it was for money, then it was for sex. Finally, it came down to blackmail. She was pregnant and planned on telling my wife Amelia everything. So, I did the best thing for everyone involved: I skipped with Kelly. Really, it was the best thing for me. I never wanted the house with the white picket fence. I wanted exactly what I have now. Spending every day on the water. I never wanted children, not with Amelia and not with Kelly. Somehow, that wish didn't come true.

"So, Kelly, what do you want now?"

"I want you to be very nice to Benjamin's girlfriend. He never brings anyone home, so she must be special."

"What do I get in return?" Not that it matters since I was curious about her anyway. What kind of woman would make my son want to settle down?

"A blow job."

She's smiling but now I want to have fun. "Not enough, what else do you have?"

She takes her bikini top off and moves those expensive tits closer to my face.

"A blow job and I'll let you come all over these." She lifts up Thelma and Louise and tugs on her nipples. Damn, she knows how to get me.

"Deal. Get on your knees, now." I get up and drop my shorts. I'm hard as steel. I step closer and she parts her lips. I let go of my cock and let her do her thing. She has the most gifted mouth. Always warm and soft. She knows how to take me really deep. This is how I got into the mess I was in all those years ago. Blow jobs and tits—my downfall in life. It doesn't take me long and I feel my cock getting ready to explode. She rolls my balls between her fingers right before she pulls my cock out and aims it at her tits. I come all over her and when I'm done, she gets up and smiles. Like she was serving a cup of coffee. I put my cock away and continue with my fishing while she goes inside to clean herself up. Twenty years of marriage and this is what it comes down to. Everything is a negotiation, even the sex.

Brook

I'm glad I finally talked Benjamin into renting a hotel room. I'm nervous enough going to meet his parents, the last thing I want to do is worry about the whole room sharing situation. That's really the reason we didn't stay with my dad. I knew he wouldn't be ready to handle us sharing a room. Besides, it's spring break and I really need to have some fun.

"Benjamin, I want to go to the beach today. You're from here, so I'm hoping you know the best beaches to go to."

"Actually, there is a small private beach owned by a boutique hotel. My friend is a manager there and he lets me in whenever I want to. Wear your suit but bring a dress to throw over it. The restaurant in the hotel is spectacular but no bathing suits allowed."

"This sounds exciting. Are we going to your parents' house tonight?"

"Yes, I can't wait for you to meet them. Especially, my sister Jenny."

He pulls me into his arms and begins leaving a trail of kisses down my neck. "As much as I love this, if we don't leave now, we'll never get to the beach."

He groans his displeasure. "You owe me, Brook."

He gives in and I hurry up and get ready before he changes his mind. If I wanted to spend the day in bed, I could have stayed home. It would have been a lot cheaper.

When we get to the beach, it's everything I was expecting and more. The sand was like powder and the water had just the right amount of waves. Benjamin's friend made sure he had everything set up for us: lounge chairs, umbrellas, towels, and cocktails. There's a slight breeze coming off the water. I look over to Benjamin and he's sitting on his chair, facing me with a smirk that makes me tingle all over. "Can you put some lotion on my back, please?" I ask. He has a towel wrapped around him and I notice his suit is on his chair. I turn onto my stomach while he gets up and climbs on my lounge chair. He's got one leg on each side of the chair. His cock resting on my ass. I feel him slowly untying my bathing suit top. The slower he goes, the harder I feel my nipples getting. Something so simple ignites a fire deep inside my soul. My suit has ties on each side which he swiftly unties.

"Babe, I know this is a private beach, but there are people here." He tilts the umbrella like that is going to do much.

"Who do you think might be watching us? We could put on a show for them, or we could ask someone to join us," he suggests.

"Remember my rule, I don't share . . . *ever*."

He laughs. "Just kidding, hon."

I begin to relax again, enjoying everywhere his fingers are exploring. He slowly enters me from behind as I get into a plank position. He's trying to maintain his balance while slamming into me. Hopefully the umbrella covers us enough but, in reality, I really don't care. The more we have sex with the threat of others watching, the more I think I'm becoming addicted to it. The thrill of being caught brings my nerve endings alive. "Come on, babe, give it to me harder. Are you afraid someone might hear you yell?" He begins to really pound into my pussy.

"Hard enough for you, hon?"

I don't get a chance to answer. My release takes me further than ever before. He slows down and I know he hasn't found his release. Maybe being outside really doesn't do it for him. Maybe it's just the thought of people watching, like in our apartment. He pulls out and I flip over, thinking he wants to enter me from the front, instead he pulls me up and while he pumps his cock, he puts his hand behind my head. He's pulling my mouth closer, so I slightly part my lips and let him in. It's not long before I get all the signs that he's ready to come. But I also hear a whistle blowing and it's getting closer.

"Fuck, Brook, make me come now!"

I let him hit the back of my throat and with that he finds his release. He jumps off of me and throws on his bathing trunks while tossing a towel over me. All I could do is laugh which only earns me a glare. The lifeguard runs over and threatens to have us band from the beach. Thankfully, Benjamin is a great talker. He's explaining how the passion just overcame him. I'm smiling as I slowly run my tongue across my lips. The lifeguard rolls his eyes as Benjamin's face flushes.

"Benjamin, I think you're getting a sunburn, we should probably get inside before it gets any worse." I get up with my towel wrapped around me and offer him my hand. All the while trying not to laugh. He gathers up the rest of our stuff as the lifeguard reaffirms his warning. We wave goodbye and head back to the hotel.

chapter
TWENTY-EIGHT

Amelia

THANKFULLY, THE FLIGHT WAS UNEVENTFUL. DOUG GOT the rent a car and it dawns on me he knows exactly where we are going. "Doug, how did you get Peter's address?"

"You might as well tell her the rest, Mitch; you're fucked anyway."

"Wait—what the fuck—there's more?!"

Mitch rakes his hand through his salt and pepper hair. Turns toward me and I just know this is big. Part of me wants to punch him in the face, but the other part of me wants it all. Every last secret. "Spit it out, Mitch."

"I have a friend high up at the DMV. After nine-eleven, all of the computers were linked. I gave him Benjamin's name and the state that he lives in and my friend did the rest."

"So, what's the more that you are afraid to tell me?"

"When you applied for the job with the DMV, I called my friend and he made sure you got the job."

"Oh, for the love of all that's holy! Didn't you think I could get the job on my own merits?"

"It's not that I thought you couldn't, but I knew how hard things were at the time. I knew you had a mortgage, how much your payment was. Yeah, you had a night job, cleaning offices, but there was daycare along with all the other expenses. I wasn't sure you would get financial help. I knew you couldn't sell the house until Peter was legally dead. I didn't think anyone would care what happened to you, but I cared. I wanted to make sure that you and Emma survived."

How could I hate him for trying to help me even if he had a crazy way of going about it? "Maybe you should have told me in the truth at very beginning of all of this."

"I didn't think that was an option."

"Why not?"

"I was afraid the dam that was holding back my feelings was about to burst. The lies were piling up like a house of cards about to coming tumbling down. I was not going to add adultery to it."

"Have you thought about what you are going to tell, Brook?"

"No, I don't even know where to begin."

"Might I suggest you start with the truth? You are in so deep right now, that's probably your only option."

"She keeps trying to push me toward you. Maybe I should start with why I was in a loveless marriage. Maybe I should start with you."

The realization of what he's saying hits me hard. How many lives were changed by a different path that I took. I had feelings for Mitch, but then Peter blew into my life like a hurricane. By the time I came back to reality, Peter was asking me to marry him. I just aged out of the foster care system, and he offered me stability—a home and a family. Those were my dreams, not riches or fame. I was so impressionable at that time, so how could I not say yes? When the whirlwind I was on finally slowed down, Mitch had moved on to Becky. I thought he was happy, and now I know the truth. It's amazing how one word could have changed history. What would my life be if I said no? Hindsight is twenty-twenty; however, I would do it all over again only because of Emma. She's my world.

"So, are we just going to go in balls to the wall?" I blurt.

Doug is laughing, not what I expected. "Might I remind you, Amelia, you have no balls."

"Funny, Doug, very funny. What's the plan?" I ask again. He turns down a street and pulls into a parking space. "Are we here, Doug?"

"Yeah, but let's sit tight and see who goes in and out. We've waited twenty years; we can wait a little longer."

Doug is so calm. Mitch, on the other hand, is not. I would think it's because his daughter is involved in this cluster fuck of a mess. "Doug, you need to tell your daughter the entire story before Brook tells her," I mention.

"Shit, I never thought about that. Those two are as close as sisters. It doesn't have any effect on Vanni, but I know she will want to support her best friend. I'll ask Brook to let me be the one to tell her, she will."

"You're right it doesn't have any effect on your daughter and realistically not even Brook. The only one who will really get hurt by all of this is Emma. She's the one who lost out on having a father. She's the one who will have to come to terms with the fact that he didn't want her. On top of that, she will have siblings that she didn't even know existed. It's going to be a hard pill to swallow. I would appreciate it if you would both tell your children to give me a chance to tell Emma myself. I don't care about me but she's my everything."

"I'll tell Brook not to say anything to Vanni or Emma. You have my word on that."

"Thank you, Doug." I don't have a choice but to take his word for it. I sit back and try to figure out exactly what I'm going to say to Peter. I don't want to lose my shit. I'm already the better person. I raised a great daughter. Was I that bad of a wife? Could it be I was just a challenge that he conquered and ditched? What does she have that I didn't? What was he looking for all those years ago? Self-doubt is getting the better of me. Waiting has never been my strong suit. "How much longer do we need to just sit here?!" I sound like the whiny kid who keeps asking, "*Are we there yet?*" I'm about to say the hell with waiting when a bright orange Jeep Gladiator pulls up. It's like seeing my life fall apart in slow motion. The garage door goes up and the jeep pulls in. He gets out of the driver's side and a woman gets out of the passenger side. He turns towards us and that's when I see him. A face that, other than in my dreams, I never thought I would see again in my lifetime. The past coming face to face with the present. I'm mesmerized. He's got a big house, what looks to be a trophy wife, and all the expensive toys. All of this while, I worked two jobs and struggled to put food on the table. The slamming of the car door snaps me out of it. I realize Doug and Mitch are already outside the car. I hurry up and get out, trying to keep my cool. Peter is pulling coolers from the truck. Then the woman with him is helping him hose them out. Two people going about their daily lives. Mitch takes my hand and pulls me to a stop.

"Amelia, are you sure you can handle this?"

"What are you saying, I should wait in the car? No one is going to steal my thunder, Mitch, no one. I will have my say and then I'll decide after that what direction I plan on taking this. Now, get the hell out of my way, Mitch." I pull my hand away and continue walking. As we step into the driveway, Peter stops what he's doing and looks up. He looks at Doug, then to Mitch, and finally me. The realization of who we are hits him. His face instantly pales. He slowly starts toward us. When we are close enough, I whisper, "You bastard, you really are alive."

Before he can say anything more, Doug takes a swing at him and Peter quickly moves out of the way. However, he never saw Mitch's fist coming at him from the other side. He hits him square in the jaw. He's rubbing his jaw and Mitch is rubbing his knuckles. The woman, that I'm assuming is Peter's wife, steps closer to him and pulls him back.

"Peter, why don't we take this inside. We don't need all the neighbors coming out or for one of them to call the police." She stresses the word police. Peter broke a lot of laws and if the truth comes out, her gravy train just came to a screeching halt.

"Please, my wife is right. Let's not make a scene out here." He turns and heads into the garage, while we all follow. The interior garage door leads into a laundry room and then a massive kitchen with a great room. This enrages me. I know it shouldn't, but I'm only human after all. I'm thinking of everything my daughter missed out on. Then again, my daughter grew up in the real world. She didn't live her life based on a lie.

"Why don't we sit in the family room to talk. I'm sure everyone has a lot of questions." None of us move, our feet planted. I feel a rage growing inside of me that I've never felt before.

"Okay, have it your way. Who wants to go first?"

Mitch steps forward and I watch Peter make a fist, no doubt preparing for another blow.

"Peter, I'm not going to hit you. I needed to get twenty years of frustration and anger out of my system. You know I'm not that kind of man. Let's start at the beginning. Why did you skip and how did you do it?"

His wife steps up next to him and puts her hand around his waist. Like she's staking her claim.

"I skipped with my wife Kelly. She was pregnant at the time and I felt it was best for everyone involved. Actually, skipping was very easy. I met Kelly in Bensonhurst. We torched my car and drove away in hers. At first, I kept using aliases but then I realized no one was looking for me. When Kelly went into labor, I wanted to make sure that my name was on the birth certificate, not some alias I made up. After all, she was giving me a son, something Amelia wasn't going to give me. After Benjamin was born, Kelly and I got married and that was it. No big deal."

I can feel a flush coming over me. I'm not usually a confrontational person, but right now all bets are off. "She was pregnant! What about me? I was seven months pregnant with your daughter. How was being alone best for us? You married her, thinking it was no big deal, but you're a bigamist!"

"Amelia, I really thought you would have figured this out by now. I married you to spite Mitch. I knew he wanted you and I was pissed that he always got what he wanted. I figured you're a strong enough person—hell, you survived foster care. I figured you'd find a way. After all, I did leave you the house with a little surprise stashed inside. I'm sure that came in handy. So, you see it was a win-win for everyone. As far as a bigamist, that's only on paper. At first, I didn't want any children, but then I realized I really wanted a son, Amelia. They can help bring in an income. Daughters are a waste of time. Look at my daughter Jenny, she is more interested in school and boys, not bringing in some money to this house."

At this moment, I'm wrestling with my conscious. Part of me wants to kill him and the other part is telling me to walk away, he's just not worth it. "Peter, I have no idea what you left me or even where it is. Whatever it is, I don't want it or need it. I raised *my* daughter on my own. She's a good, honorable young lady, no thanks to you and your lies. You can keep your *other family.*" Filled with a rage I never knew I was capable of, I reach back and swing at him. My fist connects with the side of his throat and he stumbles backward. I've never hit anyone in my life, yet, for the second time in one day, I've hit someone. Kelly comes at me but Doug steps in between us.

"Kelly, I know you have a stake in all of this, but Amelia has a bigger one. She's waited twenty years for answers. Answers that she has a right to, so back the fuck off."

Peter steps in front of Kelly and pushes Doug aside.

"Wow, you really have no idea what I'm talking about. Amelia, I left you a couple of diamonds. I left them behind one of the panels in the drop ceiling in the bathroom. You were always talking about how you wanted to renovate it, so I thought you would find them soon enough."

"You're pathetic, do you know that? I wasn't thinking about renovating anything, I was thinking about how I was going to keep a roof over our head. I was living paycheck to paycheck. I was drinking lemon water so I could focus on having food for Emma. I worked two jobs so we could survive."

"Well, if things were that bad why didn't you just sell the house?"

I'm so mad that I'm shaking. I can't even dignify what he is saying with an answer that doesn't tell him to just fuck off and die. Mitch takes a few steps toward Peter, and I'm hoping they don't start fighting. I don't think I could take any more.

"Peter, you're a total selfish idiot. Amelia couldn't sell the house because your name is on the deed with hers. You would have had to sign the house over to her. You vanished in the middle of the night, never to be heard from again. Oh no, wait, I'm wrong; we realized two days ago that you were alive. Do you want to know how? Don't answer that, I will. My daughter's name is Brook. Is that ringing any bells for you?" He grabs Peter by the throat and pins him up against the wall. Realization hits him as his face pales, and his body slumps. His wife Kelly lets out a gasp.

"That's right, Peter, your son is living with my daughter. I hope you know I will fight that union with everything I've got. My daughter will know everything you've done, and I mean *everything*. Not only will she have no respect for you, but I will make sure she understands that the same blood that runs though you also runs through Benjamin! I will expose you for the cheating two-faced thief and deadbeat dad you really are. I'll watch you burn in hell before I let you or anyone in your family near my daughter!"

He's about to go on when I notice Brook in the doorway with Benjamin. "Mitch, stop. Brook is here." I don't know how much she's heard but it must have been a lot. Tears are running down her cheeks.

"Brook, honey, I'm sorry. I can explain everything," he says in desperation, his face is pale.

"Why are you even here? How did you know where Benjamin lived?"

"Remember I told you about my best friend Peter who disappeared in the middle of the night, leaving Amelia alone and pregnant? Well, say hello to Peter, Benjamin's father."

Brook begins to shake and sob. Benjamin tries to pull her into his arms, but she's looking at him and back to Peter before she races into her father's open arms. While Mitch is trying to comfort his daughter, Doug finally finds his opportunity to say what he has to say to Peter.

"Nothing you can say to me would ever explain why you did what you did. Where are the jewels?"

"Oh, Doug, you were always the level-headed one. I sold most of them and invested what I got for them. I held out a few pieces for my kids. The rest is . . . *gone*."

"Gone where, Peter? I want what I'm due, what we're all due."

He waves his hand around as if he needs to make a point.

"Twenty years of living expenses. Investments in start-ups

that flopped. My current business, the Diamond Reef food boat—fitting name, don't you think? My kids' education. Stuff, Doug. Besides, what are you going to do, go to the police? You have no proof we were ever involved in the robbery."

"You want proof, well I've got the photo with the jewels, remember that?"

"That's not proof. Besides, who would believe you? The internet is a wonderful thing, Doug. You should try using it. As far as anyone in Cannes is concerned, the heist never happened. You'd look like an old fool, spinning tall tales."

I'm listening to him list all the reasons the money is gone, and I really don't give a shit that is until he mentions his kids' education.

"Your kids' education! My daughter has student loans like most people in the world. Last week I was finally able to declare you dead and collect on your life insurance policy, she was going to pay off those loans. Now she will have to give it all back. You might be legally dead, but I will not be a part of insurance fraud."

"You see, Amelia, that's why I knew I couldn't tell you about the heist. You were always Miss Goodie Two-shoes. Kelly and I have had a great life, she didn't care where it came from, only where it's going."

Brook has finally calmed down. Benjamin looks shell shocked. Mitch is doing whatever he has to do to protect his daughter. Doug is clearly furious that everything is gone. Peter and Kelly are happy. And then there is me. The closure I thought I would get doesn't exist. You can't get closure when the answers are nothing but lies. Benjamin finally comes out of his daze, but his blue eyes seem dull.

"Dad, where is Jenny? I don't want my sister finding any of this out from these people." He waves his hand around everyone in the room. He seems as blindsided by all of this as the rest of us.

"She's at cheer and will be home shortly. Besides, I think we are done here. I have nothing to offer anyone here. It's best if you all leave, now."

I don't think I can tolerate any more of his lies and his cocky attitude. I look to Doug and then to Mitch with Brook. "I think it's best if we all leave. We don't need anything from him. If anything, he needs us to keep our mouths shut. Come on, Brook, I think it's best if we go back to our hotel for now." Peter's jaw is tight and there is a slight tic. I reach my hand out toward her and she takes it. She looks over at Benjamin and begins to sob again. I wrap her in my arms as I would my own daughter.

"Benjamin, I need some time. I'll call you."

We head out the way we came in, leaving Peter to wonder what we will do next.

chapter
TWENTY-NINE

Brook

THE RIDE TO THE HOTEL ROOM WAS VERY QUIET. UNCLE Doug focused on the road in front of him. Daddy lets out a long low sigh as he stares out the window. Amelia is looking down at her wringing hands. She's the one who has to be hurting the most.

"Brook, we need a favor. I know you're upset and want to talk to your best friend, but can you please wait. I need to get to Emma and tell her the truth myself."

Oh my gosh, Emma has a father that's alive. It's the one thing she talked about with me and Vanni. How she wished she could have experienced father-daughter dances, dates, and all the things that a father-daughter would do. "Amelia, I promise I won't say a word to anyone. If you want me to go with you, I will."

"Thank you, but I don't think that will be necessary. Doug, can you drop me off at the airport. I want to head to Illinois right away."

"By this time, there are no more outbound flights. I already booked a hotel room. Let's check in and get some sleep. We can book your ticket tonight."

"Okay, besides I need to figure out how I'm going to explain all of this to her. I was tossed into foster care at a very young age. I know what it feels like to know you're not wanted. How do I explain it to Emma that it had nothing to do with her? She was always loved and wanted. Nothing that happened tonight will ever change that." Amelia closes her eyes and begins to cry so hard that she now has the hiccups. I take her hand and try to offer her some comfort. The rest of the ride is in silence.

We get two rooms: one for Amelia and I and the other for Dad and Uncle Doug. There is an adjoining door which we have open for now. Both rooms are suites with a small kitchenette, table and chairs. Now comes the hard part—I need to know everything from beginning to end. I just don't know how much my father is willing to tell me. He's a very reserved person. If he did something he's ashamed of, he won't say anything. Amelia is lying in bed, not crying or sleeping. She's staring into space. Maybe it's shock, maybe we should call a doctor. I head into Daddy's room.

"We need to talk about Amelia," I announce. Uncle Doug puts his beer down, gets up from his chair, and pulls me further into the room. He partially closes the door while daddy is still picking at the label.

"Brook, she was dealt a major blow today. Hell, we all were. Let's just give her some time."

"Uncle Doug, she's in a catatonic state. At least call a doctor to look at her."

"I promise you, if she's like this in the morning, I will take her to the hospital myself, okay?"

"Okay, in the meantime, you both have to tell me everything." I take a beer and sit down next to Daddy at the table. He gives up on the label and pushes it away.

"I know you deserve the truth. I'll tell you everything, but please understand I was a different man back then, we both were."

"Okay, Daddy, I will listen."

"You already know that the three of us grew up together. Times were so much different back then. Every chance we got, we pushed the envelope a little bit further. One of those times changed all of our lives forever. We went on spring break to Cannes, France. We partied day and night with a very wild crowd that Peter had hooked us up with. One night, we had way too much to drink and that's when Peter hatched a plan to rob a high-end jewelry store in an elite hotel. Looking back, it's easy to say *what the hell were we thinking*. However, back then, it was like a dare we couldn't pass up. Honestly, we got away with it and to this day, I'm not really sure how. We came back to the States three very rich kids. We each took turns hanging on to the jewels until the heat died down. During that time, Peter took the jewels, staged his death and left a very pregnant Amelia behind." Uncle Doug reaches into his pocket, pulls out two pictures and puts them down in front of me, along with a very faded newspaper clipping.

"When you showed up with Benjamin, we realized the secret we kept hidden from everyone for twenty years just came home roaring to the surface. Now we have to deal with the repercussions that go along with it. That's the gist of the story." I'm trying to absorb everything he's telling me, but I can't take my eyes off the photos.

"I'm sure you are omitting some of the details for my benefit. That being said, you need to understand that I love Benjamin. I can't blame him for what his father did, the same way he can't blame me for what you did."

"What if he knew, think about that one. You and Vanni knew nothing; that's the way we wanted it. Hell, Amelia only found out after you left to come here. It was all kept very hush hush for a reason. The more people that knew about it, the more we took a chance on getting caught."

"Why didn't you help Amelia out? I mean Peter was your friend and his wife needed the help to survive." I'm looking from Uncle Doug to my dad. Uncle Doug finally turns away.

"I know you want the truth. I've never said this to anyone, but maybe this will help you understand more. Peter brought Amelia around and I was instantly attracted to her, but I was very shy. Peter knew that and took advantage of it. After everything that happened tonight, I realize, to him, it was just a game. He swept her off her feet and I was left in the dust. I loved her, but she married him. I knew if I helped her after he left, I would get involved with her. I have morals and values that I was not willing to compromise. I thought I was setting an example for you. But when you told me you didn't want to be in a marriage like mine, it hit me hard. I tried to do everything right but only ended up doing everything wrong."

My heart breaks for him and Amelia, but I still don't feel like he's telling me all of it. "I know there's more, Dad. You might as well tell me now, cause if I find out later, I'm going to be really pissed." I'm looking at Uncle Doug and now I know I'm right.

"Mitch, you might as well tell her, she's going to find out anyway when she compares stories with Vanni." He mutters under his breath something about stupid ideas biting them in the ass.

"We were planning the trip to Cannes for almost two years. I got my real estate license. I sold houses and if the houses needed repairs Doug would do them. We would lift some stuff from each house. Not enough to get caught, but enough to add to the vacation fund. Peter would sell the stuff at pawn shops."

"You're my dad, the man my friends all called Dudley Do Right. Now you're telling me you are nothing but a common thief!"

"Actually, Brook, look at that clipping I showed you. Your dad, Peter, and I were anything but common. The heist was valued at sixty million dollars and that was in 1996. I don't even know by today's standards what the value would be."

"This is such a fucked-up mess. How many lives were destroyed because the three of you built your lives on a house of cards ready to tumble? I'm getting tired of asking this; is there anything else that you're not telling me?"

"Doug and I have a holding company that buys and sells properties. We use that for our flipping homes business. We purchased Amelia's house so we could tear it apart looking for the diamonds. I told Amelia about it when I told her the truth about everything."

"Well I guess now it's up to the kids to pick up the pieces. I need to see Benjamin, Dad. I need to know what he knew and when. I also want to be there for Emma. I'm sure she will want to meet her father."

"What will you do if he knew all or even some of this and didn't mention it?"

"Well, unlike you, I will not have a relationship based on a lie." I toss my empty bottle into the trash as I take my raging headache to bed.

chapter
THIRTY

Benjamin

EVERYONE LEFT BEFORE JENNY GOT HOME. I TRIED TO follow what my dad was saying: his best friends, France, diamonds, two wives, and a half-sister. I was so blown away. This is a lot to throw at someone. It's like a soap opera or a movie on Netflix. I want to be the one to tell Jenny. My dad never wanted her. He said girls are useless until they are older, and my mom only had her to try and keep my dad around. He's made it known that he does his share of wandering around. I think it's disgusting, but I have Jenny to worry about. She's the reason I come home. No one cares about her, only me. Someone has to be in her court. I warned my mom and dad not to say anything to her. I'll take her back to the hotel with me. I'll be the one to tell her. My dad's response was "good" my mom's response "it's for the best." That's the loveless home that she is growing up in.

Brook: I'm at a hotel with everyone. It was a rough night. We need to talk Can you meet me?

Me: I'm at our hotel. I've got my sister with me. I couldn't leave her there. I told her everything I found out but I'm guessing you found out more. Would you mind if she was here? Jenny and I really need to hear it all.

The three little dots are flashing while she types her response. I wonder if whatever else she found out ends up destroying our relationship? Maybe she's going to end it with me. All because our parents are fuck ups.

Brook: Okay. I'll see you soon.

"Hey, Benjamin, is everything okay?"

"Jenny, I'm hoping it will be. Brook is coming over to talk," I say with a sigh. She puts a tray down in front of me. Two Starbucks venti coffees and a slice of lemon pound cake. While she sits next to me, mindlessly eating her cake, I notice how tired she really is. Last night I dumped everything on her. It took all night, but I think we somewhat came up with a plan.

"Do you think Mom and Dad will go along with your plan?" she states as if reading my mind.

"All we can do is try. I know it will be hard for you, but we really don't have very many options."

"They never hid the fact that they never wanted me. That's why I worked so hard in school to skip a grade. The sooner I get done, the sooner I can get out of there."

"I know and I'm so proud of you but, unfortunately, you'll only be seventeen when you graduate. That's your biggest problem. I promise you, though, that I won't leave you behind, no matter what." There's a knock on the door and then it opens. I thought it was housekeeping but it's Brook. She looks just as tired as the rest of us.

"Good Morning, Brook. This is my sister, Jenny." Jenny is a hugger and I think Brook is taken back by her boldness.

"I'm going to go down to the pool, give you guys some privacy."

With Jenny gone, I take Brook's hand and lead her to the cafe table on the balcony. The warm sunshine is a welcome change from Boston. "So, Brook, maybe you should go first. I'm sure you know a lot more than I do."

"That's just it, Benjamin, I need to know how much of this you knew."

"None of it, that's the scary part. I've been reliving every day of my life, trying to see what I missed, but I've drawn a blank. Even after everyone left yesterday, no one would talk to me. When Jenny came home, we left and came here. I didn't want my parents to tell her anything. I needed to be the one to do that."

"Why you?"

"This is painful to say out loud, but I love you and trust you with my life. My dad never wanted Jenny. When she was old enough, my mom told her that she should have gotten an abortion, but she thought Jenny was a good insurance policy to keep my dad around at least until she was eighteen. It's a terrible feeling to know that you're unwanted. She worked hard in school, skipped a grade, and she graduates in June. The problem is, because of when her birthday is, she started school early. Add to that, she skipped a grade; she will only be seventeen when she graduates. I can't leave her with them after graduation, I just can't. If I have to change my life around, I will."

"I need you to know that I also knew nothing. I sat my dad down last night and he told me everything. Some of it is very sad and some of it is bizarre. The question is, how do we all move forward after this?"

"I love you, Brook, and nothing that has happened will change that. I can tell you I want nothing to do with my parents. Like I said, I plan on having Jenny live with me when she graduates high school in June. She has no choice; she has to stay with my parents until then. After I graduate in May, I will hopefully nail a job, along with a place to live. Wherever that is, I need to make sure I have a place for Jenny. I hope you will be okay with that." She gets up and climbs into my lap and wraps her arms around me.

"I love you, Benjamin. Everything I found out last night is their past, not mine and not yours. The person I feel sorry for is Emma. She is a very sweet girl. Now she has to deal with a father who isn't dead. She went from being an only child to having two siblings. On top of that, she needs to support her mom through all of this. Amelia, like us, knew nothing, not even the fact that my father has been in love with her all these years."

"Jesus, I didn't even think about the fact I have another sister. Maybe I need to take Jenny and go meet Emma."

"Please hold off on that. Amelia left today to go tell Emma everything. I promised her Vanni and I would wait until we talked to her about it."

"Okay, I can understand that. Would it be okay with you

to wait to tell me what you found out? I would like Jenny to be here. I'll call her to come back up from the pool." She agrees and I quickly call Jenny. Ten minutes later, she comes through the door.

"Brook, I appreciate you taking the time to explain to us everything you've learned. I'm sure it was painful for you, as it will be for us."

"Jenny, I can only tell you what my dad and Uncle Doug told me. It's their point of view. Maybe you should speak to your dad to find out his side of the story."

"Apparently, with the little bit my brother has told me, my dad is a liar and a thief. I wouldn't trust anything he has to say."

"I told her what little I could get out of my parents last night. But, like she said, we can't trust anything they told me."

Brook begins the story, starting way back before we were even born. Jenny and I don't interrupt her although our eyes widen at some of the things she's telling us. It's actually surreal to think our fathers were thieves. When she finally finishes, I reach over and lift Jenny's chin that's practically on the ground. She is in shock, but I'm speechless.

"Benjamin, I'm going back to Boston tomorrow. I want to be as far away from this as possible. Jenny, you are welcome to stay with us for as long as you need."

"Thank you, that's very kind. What happens next with them? I mean they robbed that jewelry store. They pilfered jewelry from homes. The life insurance money has to be returned along with the money from social security. Once that happens there will be a lot of questions and, possibly, criminal charges. I mean my father is a bigamist, that's against the law. He can go to jail for that. After Benjamin told me last night,

I looked it up and he can get five years and a fine. My mother knew it, so she can be charged, too. All of this leaves me wondering if he has ever lived within the law?"

"Brook, Jenny wants to be an attorney, as if you couldn't tell. But she does have some valid points. What's going to happen to them?"

"I have no idea. My dad said your dad blew through all the money he got for the jewels. Well, all except for a couple of diamonds that your dad hid in Amelia's house before he skipped."

"And this." I reach into my pocket and pull out a ring. Jenny gasps, no doubt at the size of it. Brook is glaring at me.

"Please, Brook, don't look at me like that. I have no idea if this is part of the jewels. Knowing what I know now, I would venture to say yes. When I told my parents that I wanted to bring you home for them to meet. My dad asked me if you where the one, the one to make me say the L word. When I said yes, he gave me this ring and told me it was my great-grandmothers. He said it was the only thing he had from his family. He wanted me to have it to give to you." I put the ring down in front of her. The center stone is a beautiful blue diamond surrounded by white diamonds.

"I would have said yes without the ring. If it really is from your great-grandmother, then you should hang on to it. If it's from the robbery, I don't know what to tell you to do with it. Uncle Doug had an article from a French paper with the information about the robbery. I had to recall my high school French, but it looks like at first the robbery was reported, after that, it could not be proved. I'm paraphrasing because I never was very good in French anyway."

"At the end of the day, we have to pick up the pieces from our parents screw-ups. It shouldn't be; we should learn from them. Do you know what Amelia is going to do after she tells Emma?"

"Whatever she does, she needs to figure her way out of it without implicating herself. She already said she didn't want anything to do with the diamonds hidden in her house. Besides, technically it's no longer her house; my dad and Uncle Doug purchased it."

"Knowing my parents, they will do nothing. My dad will drop the ball in everyone else's court. He'll never take responsibility for any of this. I think the best thing to do is leave all of this behind. I decided tomorrow I'm going to go back to Boston with you. Jenny, you've got four months to graduation. I'm going to leave the choice up to you, providing everything at home is status quo."

"Well, at least we have some sort of plan. I will keep in touch with Amelia and find out when you both can meet Emma."

That's something I'm going to have to gear myself up for.

chapter
THIRTY-ONE

Amelia

THIS IS BY FAR ONE OF THE HARDEST THINGS I'M GOING have to do. I don't even know where to begin since I don't understand it myself. Thankfully, Emma only has one class today. By the time I get from the airport to her apartment, she'll be home. As promised, Brook called me after she spoke with Benjamin. I was happy that he knew nothing about the nightmare his father has created. She said that Peter didn't want Jenny, but Kelly had her as a way to try and keep Peter around. Although, Brook said it didn't keep Peter from running around with other women. Sadly, the only kid he wanted was Benjamin. As messed up as this situation is, at least these kids have their heads on straight. Emma is strong, but I don't care how strong you are, it's going to hurt knowing you weren't wanted by your own father. I pull up just as Emma gets home.

"Mom, what are you doing here?"

"Let's get inside; I have a lot to talk to you about." As we head inside, I'm trying to get my nerve up while remaining calm. She instantly starts the tea kettle. It's our thing whenever we need to talk. A cup of tea and a box of tissues.

"Okay, Mom, tell me what's going on. You look very pale, and your making me nervous. Is your health okay?"

"My health is fine. We've always had a pact to tell each other the truth, no matter what. I do have a story to tell you, and it's almost like a movie, a really bad movie." I take a deep breath, slowly exhaling. "I found your dad, Emma. He's alive." I see the wave of shock and confusion come over her face. I take her shaking hand in mine to offer her some support.

"He's not dead? Where has he been? Why didn't he contact us? How did you find him?"

She's peppering me with questions. I understand why, but I need a moment. "Please, slow down and I'll tell you everything I know. This is where the story gets crazy." She tries to take a sip of her tea, but her hand is shaking so bad she gives up.

"He's not a nice person, Emma. He's married to someone else. Her name is Kelly. He has two children, Benjamin and Jenny. The kicker is Benjamin is Brook's boyfriend."

"Wait, our Brook? Did she know?"

"No, none of the kids had any idea. But there's a lot more." I go on to explain about the robbery, the diamonds hidden in the house. Plus, the fact that Mitch and Doug now own our house.

"I can't believe all of this. It's such a bizarre story."

I want to skip over the bad parts, but I promised her the truth. "A story that we are living in. Sadly, there's still more. Your father said he married me because Mitch was in love with me. He didn't want me, but he didn't want Mitch to win. Peter was having an affair with Kelly and got her pregnant while I was pregnant with you. He skipped town with her and later on married her. It's sick and very twisted."

"So, not only is he a lowlife deadbeat father, but he's a crook and a bigamist. I can't believe Mitch was involved with the robbery and the scam. He seemed like a nice enough guy that wanted to help you out. It's so obvious he still has feelings for you. Did you talk to him about all of this?"

"Of course, I did. I'm just as shocked as you. He said he was sorry for all the secrets and lies. He stayed away because he basically had no will power and, since he was married, he thought it was best. A crook with morals and values, imagine that." I scoff. She becomes very quiet, seemingly taking a moment to absorb all of this in.

"Tell me about my siblings," she finally speaks up again, "Do they want to meet me? What about my father? Does he have any interest in me at all?"

Even though I'm trying to be strong for her, it still hurts me so much. "I spoke to Brook this morning and she said the first thing out of Benjamin's mouth was 'when can we meet Emma?' As far as your father is concerned, can I ask you why you want to meet him? He couldn't stay around and meet you when you were born, why bother now?"

She pulls a tissue out of the box and dabs at her eyes. "I need to show him that I'm a better person, not because of him, but because of you. He is nothing more than a sperm donor. To think I wanted a brother or sister my entire life and now I find out that I have both. I want to meet them sooner rather than later. We may never end up close but, as an only child, it would be nice to have a family."

"I never thought of it that way. All I have is you and Chloe; you're both the only family I need. I only ask you for one thing. When you are ready to meet them, I would like to be there." I don't trust him, and I need to protect her at all costs.

"Mom, you know I'm an adult and can take care of myself. That being said, I don't have a problem with you being there, but it's not just up to me. Everyone would need to agree."

"I'm so proud of you, Emma." I hardly get the words out before she pulls me into a hug. I can feel her body shake with her sobs. My heart breaks for her all over again. "Emma, I know this is a complete shock for you—for all of us—but please don't look back and think about what you missed not having a father in your life. Seeing who he is today, I doubt he would have been the storybook father you've dreamed about having." Her sobs finally stop.

"Mom, have you decided what you're going to do about Mitch? Is it true that he was in love with you all that time? Did you love him?"

"Other than move, I haven't decided what I'm going to do. When your father and I started dating, it was a whirlwind. I realize now that is what Peter wanted. He caused a major distraction for me. You've got to remember, at the time, I was only seventeen. I never gave myself a chance to explore my feelings for Mitch. I blinked and I was married."

"Will you give yourself a chance to explore those feelings now?"

I finish the last of my tea as I think about what she's asking. "No matter how many different ways you ask me, I still don't have any answers. Hell, I don't even know if he's going to go to jail. All of this is so new and upsetting, I need time to digest it all before I make any other decisions."

"What about the diamonds?"

"What about them? I don't want them. Besides, they are in Mitch and Doug's house now. One thing less that I have to deal with."

"But you are still keeping the proceeds from the house, right?"

"Oh, hell yeah. I paid that mortgage and maintained that investment for twenty plus years. I legally earned every penny, not like Peter."

"Mom, why not keep the diamonds? We lived for so long with so little. You know, finders keepers and all."

"Emma, that would make me no better than them. I rather work hard to achieve my dreams then do it on the back of a crook. Think about it for a minute. Would you appreciate anything you would gain with the stolen diamonds?"

"No, I get it. Besides, you always told me bad follows bad. How is Brook holding up with all of this? I mean, her dad and her boyfriend, that's got to be a lot. Did anyone tell Vanni?"

"Doug wants to tell her himself, which I totally understand. As far as Brook is concerned, she is dealing with this better than I thought she would. I think the fact that Benjamin knew nothing helps."

"I'll check up on her later. In the meantime, I think I'd like to go meet my father."

I'm not a religious person, but I close my eyes and say a prayer that she's as strong as she thinks she is. I know one thing—I need to talk to Chloe. While Emma packs, I decide to call her. She picks up on the first ring.

"It's about time you decided to call me. What the hell is going on?"

"Calm down; I'll tell you everything. But first, how's Rusty?"

"The big lug doesn't want to get out of my bed. I think you're going to have a fight on your hands when you come to take him home."

"You might want to sit down for this one. I found Peter. He's alive, married with kids." I hear the phone drop.

"Hello, Chloe, are you okay?"

I hear rustling. "Sorry, I dropped the phone. Are you serious?"

I go on to explain the whole story. All I hear are her constant "no fucking ways" and "what a shit he is."

"Amelia, I really don't want to dump anything more on you, but I've been thinking about this since Mitch came back into the picture. I was seeing Doug. It ended abruptly when I found him in bed with his now wife. It was in my past and I didn't think it was a big deal since they never came around."

I don't think she purposely hid this from me. I know her, and she must have a good reason. "Why are you telling me this now?"

"I want you to understand the type of people you're dealing with. It was over before you and I even met. I went to see

Doug the other day with Rusty. Truth be told, I was hoping Rusty would have bit him in the balls, but no such luck. Before you ask, I went to warn him that Mitch better not break your heart. I felt that he knew something and when I called him on it, he brushed me off. Now it all makes sense."

I know no matter what, she will always have my back. "I need to figure out what I'm going to do about Mitch."

"Before you do that, you need to find out what they are going to do about the crimes they committed. That will tell you what to do about Mitch."

Emma comes out of her bedroom with her backpack. Oh, to be young and fit my whole world into a backpack. "Chloe, Emma's ready; I've got to go. I'll call you after she meets Peter. Love you and hug Rusty."

"Love you, too. Be careful."

She takes one look around before she locks the door, and we head to the airport.

chapter
THIRTY-TWO

Mitch

BAD THINGS ALWAYS HAVE A WAY OF COMING BACK TO bite you in the ass. The mistakes of my past have not only messed up my future but has put a major crack in my relationship with my daughter. I preached to her to live a good, honest life, yet, I did everything the opposite. Live what you preach should have been my motto. Instead, it was do as I say not as I do. First, I have to fix my relationship with Brook. Then, I need to figure out how I can fix everything with Amelia. Doug already left to confess everything to Vanni. She's a tough kid and will take him to task. Before I do anything, I need to talk to Peter. I need to know what his plan is. Before Doug left, I asked him what he wanted to do. We could retrieve the diamonds and turn ourselves in. Or we could retrieve the diamonds, sell them, and donate the money to charity. Amelia already said she wants nothing to do with the diamonds. A lot of people know the truth, but no one can prove it without the diamonds. I know for a fact that Peter would never go to jail. Maybe I should ask the kids what they want us to do. They've had their heads screwed on straight since day one. My phone is ringing but I'm not sure what I did with it. I finally find it between the seat cushion, but I missed the call. It was Amelia. I quickly call her back.

"Hey, sorry I missed your call."

"Emma and I are at the airport. We are taking a flight to Jacksonville. Emma wants to meet her father. She wants to surprise him on the hope that he won't run away. Where are you?"

"I'm still in Jacksonville. I was going to go see Peter before I fly out of here. I'm not sure what to do. What he expects us to do. Let Emma know that Benjamin, Brook, and Jenny went back to Boston. Do you want me to wait for you?" I hope she wants to see me. That would be a start towards redemption.

"Yes, I don't want him to bolt. Emma wanted to make sure Brook was okay. She'll probably go up to Boston to check on Brook and meet Benjamin and Jenny after she meets Peter."

"I think that would be for the best. Let her handle things on her timeline. I can pick you up at the airport if you would like." Her silence sets my nerves on end.

"Yes, I think that would be great."

"Okay, text me your flight information. Have a safe flight."

"Thank you." And with that, she hangs up.

I'm in a panic. I need to figure out not only what I'm going to say to her but also to Emma. I need to try and win over Amelia's heart and show Emma I'm not a bad person, just a man who made some bad choices in life.

Emma

I'm sitting on the plane, putting on a brave face. However, I'm anything but brave. What do I say to someone that never wanted me? Someone who is so shallow that he only wanted boys. I already have a job lined up right after graduation, a good paying, legitimate job. Thankfully, I didn't inherit anything from him.

I'm watching my mom trying to figure out what she should do about Mitch . . . about all of this stuff that she's been thrown into.

"Mom, why don't you let me help you."

"Thank you, but I think everything depends on what can they go to jail for? What can the police prove? We are returning the insurance money. I will not be a part of any crime. Did you cash the check?"

"No, truthfully, I kept staring at it. I knew if I cashed it, then I would be admitting that he was dead. That would be so final. I know that must sound crazy, but my dream has always been to find out my dad was alive. That he was kidnapped or lost his memory, anything but this. I honestly don't know how to deal with being unwanted. You, Chloe, and all my friends always made me feel wanted. I don't want to sound mean, but how are you dealing with it?"

"It's not easy. I was very young and very inexperienced when I met him. I don't think I really got to know him. Truthfully, growing up the way I did, I learned at a very young age not to put your trust in anyone but yourself."

"If that's the case, then why aren't you bitter?"

"At the end of the day, you have a choice. Let it make you a bitter cold person or give others the benefit of the doubt. I chose to not let it make me bitter. I raised you to see the positive in people but rely on yourself and no one else. That way you won't be disappointed."

"I hope I can be as strong as you."

She goes back to staring out the window while I pull out my phone and connect to the Wi-Fi on the plane. Modern technology is a beautiful thing. Although my mom doesn't think so. I hate surprises and I love research. She might not want to know what lays in front of Mitch, but I want to know. She has strong feelings for him and maybe I can help her make the right decision. First up is insurance fraud. My mom knew nothing which is easy to prove so she wouldn't be charged. My dad, however, can get up to five years in a federal prison. Bigamy in Florida is a third-degree felony with a five thousand dollar fine and up to five years in prison. Chances are he will get off with just a fine. I would be happy if they threw my father in jail. He hurt so many people, let him see what it feels like. Anyway, I don't want to become bitter.

I look up the robbery. Holy crap, this was a big deal. How did these three guys, who were around my age at the time, pull this off? The first article said they got away with sixty million in diamonds and jewels. They shot up the store but only fired blanks. The next article says the robbery was listed in the Guinness Book of World records but that it never happened, so it was pulled from the book. The proof of the crime is sitting in my mom's ceiling and the photo that my mom told me about. France does have an extradition treaty with the United States. France doesn't extradite its own citizens, well that's interesting. Even if we turn everything over to the authorities, France now has a default rule. It states that *prosecution of crimes must occur within 20 years of when the acts were committed and must be prosecuted within six years*. Well, I'll be, those fools will actually get away with the biggest crime ever. The biggest question I have is: how did they do this on their own? There had to be someone else, a silent partner. I want to share this with Mom, but she is asleep. I don't want to disturb her. I'll file this away until later.

chapter
THIRTY-THREE

Amelia

TRUE TO HIS WORD, MITCH WAS WAITING FOR US AT the curb. He takes us back to the hotel and has kept the adjoining room for us.

"Thank you, Mitch."

"You're welcome, Amelia. Emma, have you thought about what you want to say to your father?"

"I have some questions for him and for you."

He nearly chokes on his water. She never told me she had questions for him.

"Mitch, everyone is emotionally involved with everything that happened from the robbery to the bigamy, all the way down to my father's illegitimate kids. I did some research before we came here and, at the end of the day, the statute of limitations on the robbery has run out. Bigamy in Florida is a joke. He'll probably get slapped with a fine. My biggest question goes back to the crime. Was there a fourth person?"

He pulls out the picture of the three of them with the diamonds and passes it to Emma.

"Doug left it with me. You can see for yourself there is only three of us in the photo. The camera had a timer, so I was able to set it up to take the picture. There was no one else involved."

"I'm sure you believe that, but I don't."

He's about to argue with her but she puts up her hand stopping him. "Hear me out. Why did no one believe the robbery really happened? Why did it go from the heist of a lifetime to a hoax? It was pulled out of the record books and now it's one of those urban legends. Yet, right here is the proof that it did happen." She points to the diamonds in the photo. Everything happened so fast for me that I didn't even think of it. Mitch's face pales.

"I understand what you're saying, but I have no clue. Peter arranged everything. He came up with the plan . . . Oh, for heaven's sake! He had to have played us like the fools we were. I need to call Doug before he gets on the plane."

He calls Doug, pacing around the room as he waits for him to pick up. I've never seen him this pissed off. He finally hangs up and grabs a bottle of beer from the fridge.

"What did Doug say?"

"He knows nothing. He was about to get on his flight to go back to New York, but instead, he'll get a rental car and come back here. It's time we all sit down and find out once and for all what the hell happened."

"I want to confront my father sooner rather than later, but I will wait until Doug gets here. My feeling is, once he knows the cats out of the bag, he'll probably skip again. You know a leopard doesn't change its spots."

"I know you must be sitting here thinking we are total idiots, but, Emma, we were young, and we trusted each other. There was never any reason to doubt that bond. When Peter rolled right over me to get to your mother, I didn't blame him; I blamed myself. I had no confidence whatsoever. I never thought I was good enough." I'm listening to him explain the past and it makes my memories clearer. You know, when so much time passes, you tend to remember the good and the bad fades into the background.

"Mitch, I had no idea you felt so strongly about me. I really wish I did. Maybe we would have done things differently."

"No, Amelia, things are exactly as they were supposed to be. That doesn't mean we can't explore the future together."

Before I could answer him, there's a knock on the door. He gets up and lets Doug in. I remember that Emma met Vanni, but not Doug. I quickly introduce them. She pulls her shoulders back and shakes his hand.

"Nice to meet you, Emma, wish it was under better circumstances. You look just like your mother."

"Thank you, and Vanni looks just like you."

We all sit at the round table while Doug passes out cold beers. I've come to understand how much he loves his beer. "Now, Emma, please explain your theory to me about this fourth person."

"Like I told Mitch, why did it go from the heist of a lifetime to a hoax? Someone covered it up. The question is who? Find that person, and you'll find out why."

Everyone becomes very quiet. Doug is staring at the label on his bottle. Mitch is flipping his beer cap through his fingers like a poker chip. He finally stops and breaks the silence in the room. "We didn't go to Cannes to do the heist; we went to have the spring break of a lifetime. It was only when we were there that the idea for the robbery happened."

"Who came up with the idea?" Emma asks.

"Peter, did."

"Were the three of you together the entire time?"

Doug rolls his eyes and begins to laugh. "Emma, it was twenty plus years ago. We were drunk most of the time."

"Okay, point taken. Whose idea was it to go to Cannes?"

"Peter's. He had such a love for boats, that one summer, he and Mitch worked on yachts."

"Mitch, how old were you when you guys worked on the yachts and where did you go?"

He rakes his hands through his hair, which I've come to realize is a nervous habit of his.

"We were twenty years old. Peter and I worked as a team. In the beginning, it was just a weekend gig. Then one of yacht owners approached Peter and asked if we would be interested in a month-long trip. He jumped at the chance to get out of Brooklyn for a month and spend it out on the big blue sea. I was unsure but Peter said he wanted to go, and I had no choice. He promised me I would have a month I would never forget..." His voice trails off.

"Was it?"

I lean in, making sure I don't miss a word of what he has to say. He gets a melancholy look, no doubt remembering better times.

"Yes, it was. The owner's daughter was home from college. She brought three of her friends with her. Halfway through the trip, Peter was sleeping with the yacht owner's wife. I was sleeping with their daughter. It's an adventure I had with Peter that I don't regret."

I know my daughter is going to pounce all over him with a million questions.

"That's very nice but we don't have time for you to reminisce about your summer of love. Tell us about the family and friends that you spent that month with."

Mitch's eyes become wide, he gasps, reaches out and smacks Doug in the arm. "That's it!"

"That's what and did you have to smack me?"

"The family that we spent the month with—the father became the ambassador for France. They rented the yacht for the month as a celebration before they left. We tooled all around the cape. They had a son, Conrad, whom Peter became friendly with. Doug, think back, remember when we were in Cannes and Peter disappeared for a few hours."

"Yeah, he said he hooked up with one of the girls he met at the pool. Do you think that was a lie and he hooked up with this Conrad guy?"

"It makes sense. I wish I could remember his last name."

Emma reaches into her backpack and pulls out her laptop. It takes her no time to pull up a picture. She turns the laptop towards Mitch.

"A simple google search looking for the French ambassador at that time period when you were working on the yacht. Is this Conrad?"

"Yes! That's the him. He would have looked different at the time of the heist."

"Hold on, let me check his name on Instagram. A couple of

clicks and here you go. Do either of you remember seeing this guy in Cannes?"

She turns the computer towards them. Doug's face goes pale. Mitch is staring at the photo. It's Doug's reaction that makes a chill run up my spine.

"Doug, do you know him?"

"I do." His voice is low and raspy.

"How?"

"It was after we got back. I ran into him and Peter at O'Malley's pub. I didn't think anything of it at the time. He said he was a friend, but he didn't introduce him as Conrad. It was so brief; I can't remember his name."

"Well, I venture to say that my father had inside help from the beginning. You guys just thought you pulled off the crime of the century. I hate to burst your bubble, but you've been had. He needed someone to help pull this off. Who figured out how much the jewels were worth?"

"Your father was the one who figured it out and who knew a fence to sell everything to. He's the one who said we should sit on the stuff until the heat died down. He said that way we will get more money."

"Why didn't the three of you open a safety deposit box, put everything in so all of this could have been avoided?"

"Again, your father said we couldn't trust the bank. He said the only ones we could trust was ourselves."

"I'm sure knowing what you know now, if you both look back, you will see he played you both like a fiddle." She closes her computer and puts it back in her backpack. She gets up and turns towards us. "If you're ready, I'd like to confront my father now." She heads toward the door and we quickly follow.

chapter
THIRTY-FOUR

Emma

I T'S AMAZING HOW THESE THREE MADE IT THROUGH LIFE and got as far as they got. Although, in reality, my father knew what he was doing. Mitch and Doug were vulnerable. They trusted their friendship, never thinking that a lifelong friend would do the things he's done. They say there's a sucker born every day; Peter was lucky enough to find two.

I know my mother wants to ask me what I'm going to say to my father. Truthfully, I have no idea. As a child, I wanted a father just like every other kid growing up in a single parent household. What do I need him for now? I can take care of myself; my mother was my best teacher. She wore both hats: mother and father. She always kept a positive attitude even at the lowest of times.

We pull up to the house and all the lights are out. I've got a really bad feeling. We get out and Mitch rings the bell—nothing. I try the side gate and it's open.

"I'm going around back." I don't give anyone a chance to protest. Besides, they are too busy trying to see in the windows. When I get around back, I pick up a garden gnome and smash the window on the French door. I reach in and unlock it. When I step inside, I wait to hear an alarm, but I hear nothing. I turn on the lights and look around. I find envelopes on the coffee table in the family room. They are addressed to Mitch, Doug, Amelia, Brook, Benjamin, Jenny and me. I pick them up and make my way to the front door. When I open the door, the three of them are staring at me.

"I broke the glass on the back door and let myself in. There is an alarm system, but it's not set."

"Emma, this is not like you. What happens when they come back? They are going to think I raised you with no manners."

"Mom, first of all, do you really care about what they think? Second, I don't think anyone will be coming back. He left letters addressed to everyone. Hopefully they will have the answers everyone is seeking."

I hand them each their letters. While they are deciding what to do about the letters, I keep searching around the house. The first room I hit is the master bedroom. You can tell a lot by a person's closet. Some clothes are still hanging but for the most part it's empty. There's a safe in the closest and it's open. There are some papers, so I pull them out. Most of them are legal documents for Benjamin and Jenny. There's also a copy of his death certificate. So why leave that behind?

Maybe just a dig for my mom. When I come out of the closet, my mom is standing there.

"You disappeared. Did you read your letter?"

"No, not sure I want to. Did you read yours?"

"No, I'd rather wait until I'm alone. What did you find?" She glances at the papers in my hand.

"Birth certificates and a copy of his death certificate, which is very strange. Did Mitch and Doug read their letters?"

"Yes, however, I didn't ask them any questions. If they want to tell me, they will. Mitch is going to bring Brook hers along with Benjamin's and Jenny's. He was wondering if we wanted to go with him so you can meet them."

I don't need to think long about that one. "Yes. The sooner I meet them, the sooner I can put all of this behind me. How long did they live in this house?"

"I'm not sure, why?"

"It's in very good condition, but it doesn't feel like a home. Maybe they only lived here for a short time. What about his boat? Is it possible that they are living off the boat for now?"

"Mitch thought the same thing. He wants to swing by there before we head back to the hotel."

I take the papers with me to give to Benjamin. I'm sure, at some point, he will need them. Before we head out, I check the garage to find whatever vehicles were there are gone. I'm doubtful that we will ever find them.

When we get to the boat yard, there is a security guard. He's not letting us in, so I decide to take a different approach. I pull the death certificate out of my pocket and step in front of the guard.

"Excuse me, I know you can't let us in, and I totally understand that. I mean you could lose your job and I would never want that. But do you know Peter Mach?"

"Yes, I do."

I pass him the death certificate. I watch as he reads it and realizes what it is. "You see, he's my father. He skipped out on my mother when she was seven months pregnant. I found out today that he's been alive all these years. I went to his house to meet him but once again he skipped. I need to know if he left on his boat or if it's still docked? You don't have to let me in, but if you could look, that would mean the world to me." I lay it on thick, even throw in some tears for good measure. He passes me back the certificate.

"Young lady, I'm so sorry, but he and his wife left here about an hour ago. Before you ask, he never said where he was going. I'm sorry, but that's all I know."

"Thank you for your help."

"I don't know if this will help you, but he has two boats. One is Diamond Reef, his food truck. The other one is his personal boat. He docks The Heist part of the year in the Keys."

"Wait, his boat is called The Heist?"

"Yeah, funny name for a boat. I asked him once why he named her that. He said it was a lifetime ago."

"Thank you."

We head to the car and before we climb in, Doug stops. "So, we're going to the Keys, right?"

"Doug, I plan on seeing this through to the end, whatever that may be."

My mom looks at me and then back towards Mitch. "You heard my daughter; let's get going."

We climb into the car and head out in search of my father. After looking around his house I finally figured out what I want to ask him. Why? That's it, just *why*. Why was I not worth it in your heart? After that, I'll move on.

chapter
THIRTY-FIVE

Peter

I KNOW MITCH AND DOUG BETTER THAN I KNOW MY WIFE
. . . well, my second wife, Kelly. Amelia? I never really knew
her. I married her out of spite. I know that Mitch and Doug
will be coming for me. The last thing I want to do is sit around
and wait for them. I'm not sure what the laws are but the only
evidence they have are the two diamonds. Technically, I didn't
declare myself dead and collect the insurance. That's all on
Amelia. My leaving is best for everyone. Besides, I love the
Keys this time of year. By the time they figure it out, I should
already be at my other home there.

It's a beautiful thing watching the sun come up when
you're out on ocean. It took a little longer to get here than an-
ticipated because of the weather. Thankfully, that cleared.

I pull into my slip and begin tying her up when I hear footsteps, lots of them. I turn around and holy shit—Mitch , Doug, Amelia, and a girl that must be Emma, are approaching me. She looks just like Amelia at that age. How the hell did they find me so fast? Kelly climbs off the boat and quickly comes to my side.

"Peter, how the hell did they find us?"

"Shh, let me do the talking."

When they get closer, they stop but Emma comes right up to my face. Her eyes are large; she's absolutely beautiful. "You must be Emma."

"I have one question for you and then I will leave you alone to live whatever kind of life you think will make you happy."

"Wow, that simple. Okay, ask."

"Why?"

"You're going to have to be a little bit more specific than that, little girl. Why what?"

"Why was I not worth it in your heart for you to stick around?"

"I never wanted children, but if I had to have them, I didn't want any girls. Having boys is beneficial, they can bring in some money and they won't stop working when they get pregnant. Girls are high maintenance." She stares at me and I'm sure she will start crying, because let's face it, that's what girls do. Her hand moves so fast across my face that I never saw it coming. I did, however, feel the sting of her slap.

"You are a pig, a poor excuse of a man. I found the death certificate. You knew that my mom had you legally declared dead. Did you think you were finally in the clear?"

"Actually, I did. I was pretty sure no one had the brains to think otherwise."

"Or maybe, no one really cared anymore. Thank you for leaving my mom. She's the one that taught me how to survive on my own. She taught me morals and values. She taught me to appreciate what I have. Everything else is just stuff. Stuff that will only end up on some resale site when I die. She taught me it's the memories I will leave behind that will make the most change in the world. I will never rely on anyone, especially, someone like you. You really are a pathetic excuse for a man."

I'm rubbing my cheek as she turns and walks away. Amelia follows her but not Mitch and Doug. "So, do you both want a shot at me?"

"No, we want answers, that's all. Was it Conrad who helped with the heist?"

"I'm impressed, Mitch, that you even remember him. Yes, that's why we were able to get in and out so easily. He was a manager at the hotel."

I know where this is going and I'm more than happy to tell them the truth—all of it.

"So how much was the actual total of the heist?"

"One hundred twenty million dollars. Sixty went to us. Thirty went to Conrad, twenty went to the jewelry store owner, and ten went to a local government official. We had to make those payments in order for it to work and for us to get safely out of the country."

"Why didn't you just tell us all of this at the time? Were you afraid that Doug and I wouldn't go along with the plan?"

"Honestly, Mitch, no. You're such a goody two-shoes I

mean, really, to this day, I still can't believe you went along with it. Anyway, the less people that knew, the better off we were." I don't know what else I can tell them that they don't already know. "I have nothing left, guys, so if you think I have some hidden stash, I don't. Not that you would believe me anyway."

"Why didn't you just divorce Amelia and let her get on with her life?"

Kelly pulls me closer toward her. I take a deep breath and slowly exhale.

"If I did that, you would have gone after her. It was never about her, Mitch, it was always about us."

"What the hell did I ever do to you that made you hate me so much you would destroy lives over it? How the fuck do you sleep at night?" He's screaming and his face is so red, I think he might pass out. I've never seen Mitch this mad.

"When we spent that month on the yacht, I had it really bad for Conrad's sister Melissa. Instead, I got stuck with her mother while you spent the month fucking her daughter. Oh, and for the record, I sleep like a baby."

"All of this was because of that?! You're such an idiot. All you had to do was tell me you wanted her, and I would have walked away. I walked in on you with the mother, so I thought that's what you wanted. You told me she was teaching you so much you never wanted to leave. What the hell was I supposed to think?"

"I shouldn't have to spell it out for you."

"Amelia put her life on hold for you for twenty years. Believe it or not, at some point, she actually loved you. I hope you're happy with yourself."

He turns to leave, and I know I should just shut up, but

I can't help myself. "So, Mitch, what are you going to do with the diamonds in the bathroom ceiling?" He spins back around and now he's right up in my face.

"Why, do you want them, too?"

"Maybe, if you want to give them to me." He gets a grin on his face like the cat that ate the canary.

"Well, you're too late. Brook and Benjamin went by the house before they went back to Boston. Benjamin got them out of the ceiling and Brook put them in the collection plate at Mary Queen of Heaven. I'm sure Father Francis is very excited right about now."

I'm laughing as they turn away and head up the dock to their car.

chapter
THIRTY-SIX

Mitch

I T WAS A LONG TRIP BACK TO NEW YORK. I KNOW THAT Amelia and Emma never read the letters from Peter. I don't know if they ever will. I was so impressed with Emma. Amelia really raised a great kid. I read the letter from Peter before I burned it. If I never see or hear from him again, it will be too soon. We all wanted to go with Emma to meet Benjamin and Jenny, but she wanted no part of it. She said when she feels ready to meet them, she will call. All she wanted to do was get back to school. I can understand, she's made a life for herself in Illinois and I don't think she wants any part of New York and its memories. Today is moving day, so I'm on my way to Amelia's to make sure she has no problem with the movers.

When I pull up to the house, Rusty is in the back yard by the fence freaking out. We're best friends now so I try to calm him down. I bribe him with food a lot.

"Amelia, do you want me to take Rusty back to my house until the movers are done? I'm sure your neighbors aren't too happy with him."

"I would love that. When they're done, I'll call you." She runs back inside while I put a leash on Rusty and get him in his car seat. Yep, he even has a car seat. Can you say spoiled? He loves my house, well, basically, he loves my sofa. I just start channel surfing when my phone rings. It's Brook. Since Emma decided she wasn't going to go up to Boston right away, I mailed her the letters from Peter. She got them and gave Benjamin and Jenny theirs. However, we never talked about it again.

"Hey, how's everything? How's Benjamin doing?"

"He's fine, everything is good. Today's moving day for Amelia. Are you still going to North Carolina for a while?" This is my daughter fishing, and she's not very subtle about it.

"Yes, that's still the plan. I have to help her buy a car and get settled in. Have you spoken to your mother?" Diversion is a skill.

"Yes, I told her everything. She couldn't believe it. She said she thought Benjamin looked familiar when she met him, but she didn't think much of it. How long do you think you'll be gone?"

"I'm not sure. Is there something you need?"

"Benjamin really wants to meet Emma. Do you think she would be open to it?"

"Call her and ask. If she's ready, she'll let you know."

"Okay, well, have a safe trip and text me when you get there."

"Now you sound like me."

"Love you, Daddy."

"Me, too."

We hang up and I realize as much as she'll always be my baby, she really is a beautiful woman. Benjamin called me last week and asked me for permission to ask Brook to marry him. I gave him my blessing. After everything that happened, I realize life is short and I need to be more open and flexible. I still have my crazy moments, but I figure I'm a work in progress. I'm back to channel surfing when Doug comes strolling in. We both read our letters, but we never talked about it again. I closed that part of my life. If I keep looking back, I'll miss what's right in front of me.

"Hey, what time are you leaving today?"

"As soon as the movers are done. If it's late, we'll leave in the morning."

"Have you thought about what you're going to do?"

"I don't know who's worse, you or Brook. I'm taking it one day at a time. I know I'd like to make a life with Amelia, that is, if she'll have me."

"I'm going to give you the best advice ever: get out of your own way. You've always been your biggest problem. If you want her, then go for it. Don't take a backseat to anyone."

"I know you're right. I'm trying, Doug."

He gets up and rubs Rusty's head. As he heads to the door, he turns back toward me and begins to laugh.

"What's so funny?"

"Here I am, trying to give you advice about your love life, and I'm still married to the hag—go figure!"

"Yeah, go figure." My phone pings with a new text message.

Amelia: Hey, the movers are done. I cleaned up, locked the door, and now I'm sitting on the porch waiting for you.

Me: Do you want to leave now for North Carolina or wait until morning?

Amelia: I'm so tired I'd rather leave in the morning, if that's okay.

Me: Of course. I'm on my way.

I get Rusty's leash but he's on his back fast asleep. He snores so loud he could wake the dead. I let him sleep and go out to get Amelia. I already decided that I'm going to talk to her about the future. Doug's right, I need to get out of my own way. It's time I start living my life for me. When I pull up to the house, she's sitting there with her suitcase. I swear I fall in love with her all over again. I park, get out and open the door for her. "Your carriage awaits to take you to the start of a new life."

She laughs as she climbs in and I close the door.

"I'm ready for the next great adventure. I'm glad it's starting with you," she says as soon as I get in on my side.

I think my heart just skipped a beat. When we get to the house we head inside, and I put up the tea kettle.

"Tea? You must have a lot on your mind."

"You've gotten me into the habit that whenever I want to talk, I need a cup of tea."

She curls up on the sofa next to Rusty. I come in with a tray filled with tea and cookies, put them on the coffee table and take a seat across from her. It's time I get some balls and tell her how I really feel.

"Amelia, I think you know how I feel, how I've felt for over twenty years. You know what they say, '*If wishes were horses, beggars would ride.*' I've stopped wishing and dreaming about all the what ifs. I'm putting it all out there for you. I love you. I've been in love with you for so long, I don't know any other way. I know I've done some bad things, stupid things. I know I've kept secrets, but I've laid my whole past out to you. You know every last thing about me and my past. I want to go with you to North Carolina."

"Wait, Mitch, you're already going with me, right?"

"What I mean is, I want to stay with you forever. The past few days, you've talked about putting the past behind you and moving forward. I want to move forward with you. I know I can't make up for lost time, but I want to try, if you'll have me."

"Are you serious? You want to move with me?"

"I've never been more serious in my life."

"You know I'm not going to live with a bedsheet dividing us," she jokes.

I get up and lift her into my arms as she wraps her legs around my waist. "The first thing we're going to do is burn that damn bedsheet."

She leans in and gently rubs her lips over mine. My life is no longer on hold. No more wishing and dreaming. Today my dreams are finally becoming my reality. I wanted my first time with her to be different and special, unfortunately, the urgency to finally have her takes over. She's kissing me as I carry her into the bedroom. I become so overwhelmed I nearly trip and drop her. It doesn't distract her. I know every inch of my room which is a Godsend. I gently climb onto bed and begin undressing her. I never break our contact while I quickly pull my own clothes off. We are no longer in our twenty's, but her body is spectacular. I quickly finish undressing her and start kissing her from head to toe. I'm living my dream and I'm thankful for my age. With those years comes the ability not to shoot too soon.

"Amelia, every inch of you is beautiful. How did I ever live all these years without you?"

"You weren't living, we both were just getting by. Those days, Mitch, are over."

"I'll never settle again . . . ever." I lean in and kiss her tender lips. She parts them and our tongues are doing a dance of love. I pull back again. "Open your eyes, Amelia. I want to see deep into your soul while I enter you." She opens her eyes. I pull up onto my knees and go very slowly, maintaining total control, even as she fists her hands in my hair. When I'm totally in her, I stop lean down and pull her bottom lip through my teeth. "I'm going to move now, are we good?"

"More than good, Mitch. So much more."

I start slow, making sure I give her all the pleasure she craves. She pushes her heels into my ass which pushes me harder into her. I wrap my arms around her legs and lift them higher while I slide up further on my knees, never breaking contact. I let her catch her breath before I pick up the pace. Fast and hard is all it takes to have her screaming. I feel like a freight train is racing through my blood. I start to slow down, trying to make it last even longer. She lets go of my hair, digging her nails into my arms as she nips on my shoulder. I lose it.

"Oh my God, Amelia, I love you!"

"When my heart finally starts to come down to earth, I roll off of her and tuck her into my side. I never want this feeling to end.

epilogue

Amelia

ASHEVILLE, NORTH CAROLINA, IS LIKE A DREAM. MY up-cycle business has taken off. When Mitch isn't helping me, he's wandering around with his camera. I swore I would never get married again. It was such a disaster the first time, why would I ever do it again? Well, Mitch asked me to marry him. I've lost count how many times the man had asked, and I said no. After two years, I put *The Beav* in retirement and I finally put Mitch out of his misery and said yes. I let him pick the date and made him promise to keep it simple. On a beautiful Saturday, in early June, our kids came down, along with Doug and his family. Even Chloe came down and played nice with Doug. Brook and Benjamin got married the year before and they just announced that Brook is pregnant. Jenny received an acceptance letter from John Marshall Law School in Illinois. She moved in with Emma, and they have bonded as only sisters could. Benjamin still keeps a watchful eye on both of them. He swears doing so is preparing him for fatherhood. I could not help but laugh—he's got no clue.

We tied the knot in a simple ceremony. Through all the hardship our family stepped up and blended together. We learned acceptance and tolerance. Now, we look forward to the next step in life, becoming grandparents and watching our family grow.

The End

other books

The Unraveled Trilogy

The Unraveling of Raven
Darkness into Dawn
Shattered Lies
The Bench

Unraveled: The Next Generation

The Letter: Dear Michael

Coming Soon!
Discrete Investigations

The Fitz Series

Uniquely Mine book one
Silent Innocence book two
It Will Always Be Us book three

Coming Soon!
I'm Not Your Difference

Standalone Books

Maribel's Decadent Miniatures
The Heist

acknowledgments

Wow, this year has proved life can change on a dime. Now we are all hoping for some sort of do-over. I want to take a moment to thank some people that helped make this book happen. My family and friends; with their support, I've finally been able to write again.

I'd like to give a special shout out to Kelli Smith. You've talked me through so much and held me up in the most difficult of times. You, my dear friend, are priceless.

A very special thank you to Stacey Ryan Blake of Champagne Book Design. Not only do you make my books come to life, you are there for me any time day or night.

My beta readers, Patricia Statham, Lourin Baylie Wheeler, Loraine Oliver, and Shell Reinhardt. Thank you for keeping it real.

Jacquelyn Ayres—Thelma and Louise forever. Yes, we can do it all together, against unbeatable odds.

Finally, thank you to all the readers for taking a chance on me all those years ago.

about THE AUTHOR

Theresa Sederholt is a Brooklyn, New York native turned country girl. She is a graduate of Campbell University in North Carolina, with a degree in Criminal Justice. Theresa now calls North Carolina home with her husband, a professional chef, and her two dogs.

Experiencing life first hand is what she does best. Believing she can do anything has put her in many crazy situations. Whether it's babysitting a pig farm or cutting the top off of a mini truck, nothing is ever out of reach. Her list is endless—A to Z.

Theresa's beliefs are pretty simple: there isn't a luggage rack on the hearse and with a little Nutella and espresso, a girl could change the world.

Theresa enjoys connecting with her fans. She can always be reached through her website at:

www.theresasederholt.com